Bells, Binders and Bodies

Apple Creek School District Mysteries

Book 1

Montie Red

Montie RED

ISBN: 978-1-962293-16-7

Cover design: MRed

Map Illustrator: M Red

Library of Congress

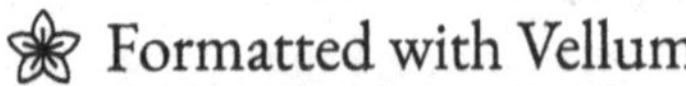

To my biggest and most interesting mystery in life, Josephine.

Apple

Creek

Mayor Demands Answers Over Missing Enrollment Study Funds

By Penelope *"Penny"* Whitcomb
Apple Creek Gazette

APPLE CREEK — What began as a routine discussion about student growth turned tense Monday night when Superintendent Harold P. Wilkins confirmed that funds allocated for a student capacity and enrollment planning study are currently unaccounted for.

The study, commissioned last year to determine whether Apple Creek requires a new elementary school, was intended to guide future construction decisions. According to Wilkins, discrepancies were discovered during a recent internal review of departmental records tied to the study's funding and reporting process.

Mayor Henry Dosal responded swiftly, releasing a statement early Tuesday. "The town council and I expect full transparency," Dosal said. "We will not rest until every dollar connected to this project is clearly accounted for."

Sources tell the Gazette that concerns were first raised weeks ago by a whistleblower within the school district who questioned enrollment figures used to justify the study's scope and cost. While Wilkins acknowledged that an audit has been requested, he declined to comment on whether those concerns influenced the timing of his disclosure.

Parents are also demanding clarity. Linda Carver, chair of the Apple Creek Parents Advisory Board, addressed officials directly. "Decisions about our children's schools must be based on accurate information," she said. "If something went wrong, families deserve honest answers."

The school board has requested assistance from the town's finance department and expects preliminary audit findings before next month's meeting. Until then, questions remain—not only about the missing funds, but about the data that set everything in motion.

Chapter 1

The moment I crossed the doors of the School District Department, I knew I was about to be bombarded with questions.

Miss Junie McCarthy was already looking up from her desk.

She was a lovely lady and a dear friend. We'd been working in this department for as long as I could remember—well, almost. Junie had only started ten years ago, which was considerably less time than me, but you get the point.

I usually enjoyed our morning coffee and a good discussion of the daily news. And what news we had today. Still, I knew Junie wouldn't care about the scandal unfolding in our department. She would be far more interested in my personal life.

She was like that.

Unlike me, who never cared much for gossip, Junie lived for it. If I ever needed to know anything about life in Apple Creek, I was convinced she'd have the answer before I even finished the question.

"Go on and have fun, Gertrude," I sighed, breaking off a small crumble and handing it to my faithful companion—and now official staff member of Apple Creek—my duck.

Thanks to Maggie Willow and an impressive amount of paperwork I still didn't entirely understand, Gertrude was now formally recognized as part of City Hall. Not that she cared much for titles, but it did mean no one could complain when she followed me into the building each morning.

She accepted the crumble with dignity, gave a single satisfied quack, and then—without so much as a backward glance—waddled toward the exit.

I watched her go, her tail swinging from side to side like she had somewhere important to be. Whether that somewhere involved the front steps, the sidewalk, or an entirely new adventure was anyone's guess.

You might think it's strange to have a duck as a pet, but it really isn't. Over the years, I'd tried to have a traditional one. The cat made me sneeze my lungs out, the dog somehow managed to leave more fur in my house than on his own body, and fish—well—fish aren't exactly known for their conversational skills.

Reptiles and rodents were never an option.

Birds, on the other hand, are brilliant. They have strong, independent personalities and tend to look after themselves. Have you ever tried bringing your dog to work, leaving him outside for the day, and trusting that he'd still be happy and exactly where you left him by the time you clocked out?

Gertrude was like that.

And I loved her quiet, steadfast company.

My hand was still on the door handle when Junie tossed the papers she was holding onto her desk and jumped to her feet, staring at me.

"Tony! Are you all right?"

I paused and looked myself over, startled by the genuine concern on her face. For a brief moment, I wondered if I was bleeding and simply hadn't noticed.

"I think so?"

Junie dropped an ice cube into the pot of a small orchid on her desk, then hurried around it and lowered her voice, even though we were the only ones in the department.

We were always the first to arrive. I hated crowds, Gertrude needed time to conduct whatever business she had outside, and Junie could never wait to escape her house and her overly needy husband, Bob McCarthy—who, now retired, had somehow become even more annoying.

"How can you be all right?" she whispered. "One thing is Wallace leaving you. But Arthur moving in? That has to be stressful, Tony."

I rolled my eyes and walked past her. Of course, she followed me into my office.

"First of all," I said, setting my bag on the desk and reaching for my coffee mug, "Wallace didn't leave me. He's traveling to Australia to help his poor brother. Remember?"

Junie nodded, then leaned closer and whispered, "But is Douglas really going to let Wallace go? We all know how hard poor Eleanor worked her whole life."

I frowned as I poured hot water into my mug. Sometimes I wondered why I talked so much with such a gossip.

"Eleanor loved not having to work, and Douglas loved her to death," I said. "He's devastated, not incapacitated. And yes—Wallace will be back in no time."

Behind me, I heard Junie exhale as she returned to her desk. "That still doesn't answer my concern about Arthur."

"Arthur is my son," I said calmly, "and he's always welcome to come—"

"And intrude on your life?" she interrupted. "Tony! You are the most peculiar person to live with, followed closely by your son. How are the two of you going to survive each other?"

I wanted to have a clever answer, like I did with my husband, but Junie was right. As much as it pained me to admit it, living with Arthur had already presented its challenges—and it had only been a weekend.

To my relief, Beatriz Wilkins stomped into the department, a newspaper clutched in her hand as she shook her head.

"It can't be serious!" she shouted. "That Penny has to be lying. My Harold would never commit such a crime."

Beatriz Wilkins's countenance was exactly what you'd expect from a woman who had just learned her husband might be implicated in fraud. I'd known her since high school, and I could count on one hand the number of times her hair and makeup hadn't been impeccably done. This morning was one of those rare occasions.

"That little skunk!" Beatriz snapped, slapping the newspaper onto Junie's desk. "Always selling red headlines. She has no proof of anything."

Junie picked up the paper and squinted at the headline.

"Mayor Demands Answers Over Missing Enrollment Study Funds."

She made the mistake of frowning and wondering aloud, "That doesn't sound so bad to me."

Beatriz's eyes nearly popped out of her head. "Are you blind? This is a clear accusation against my poor Harold!"

In all the years I'd known Junie, there was no chance she'd read past the headline. That was always my job. I read the daily news, she gathered the daily gossip, and we traded information over coffee—a routine that hadn't happened that morning, and the reason poor Junie was now on the receiving end of Beatriz's panic.

"Junie," I said, keeping my voice even. "It's not that the missing funds aren't a problem. But Beatriz is right—this Penny claims a whistleblower told the Gazette the issue was raised weeks ago and that Harold was notified about a pending audit."

"That can't be true!" Junie said. "Mr. Wilkins hasn't told me anything about an audit, and I would know. I handle the records."

Beatriz crossed her arms, then hesitated. The sharpness drained from her face, replaced by something tired. When she tried to smile, it didn't quite settle—more reflex than confidence. For a moment, it bothered me. Or maybe it was just the tension in the room getting to me. I reminded myself that people wore their fear in strange ways.

Junie was right, even if she didn't yet see what was coming. If this unraveled further, she'd be pulled into it whether she liked it or not. And while I doubted Harold had done anything illegal, I was absolutely certain Junie hadn't. She couldn't keep a secret to save her life—and committing fraud required more restraint than Junie possessed. Besides, the last thing she wanted was to stop working and be stuck at home all day.

"I'm going to sue this Penny," Beatriz said, though her voice had lost some of its bite. "Unless she has proof, she has no right to accuse anyone. This is pure sensationalism."

I wasn't entirely convinced. I didn't care much for Penelope Whitcomb's tone, but compared to some of her past articles, this one felt almost careful.

"Have you talked to Harold?" I asked gently.

Beatriz shook her head, her shoulders sagging. "No. I didn't ask him about the Monday meeting. For the first time ever, he came home upset, and I didn't push. I thought the council had denied the school funding. Yesterday he left early, came home late... and this morning he was gone before I finished getting ready. It's not even nine."

She looked suddenly smaller, less composed, and the anger from earlier made more sense. Fear had simply beaten me to the room.

Honestly, it didn't strike me as especially suspicious. Wallace used to work with the FBI, and there were days I barely saw him, much less spoke to him. Knowing Harold, he was probably buried in paperwork, trying to make sense of a situation that had spun out of his control.

"He hasn't shown up yet," Junie said. "If there really is an audit, we need to start pulling records immediately."

That, however, was a red flag. Harold should have known better. Even if he was embarrassed, there was no way he could handle this without Junie's help. She was the Records Coordinator. If the problem involved enrollment numbers and school capacity, she was essential.

"Well, we can't just sit here," I said, reaching for my purse.

"Where are you going?" Junie asked.

"I'm going to speak with the other person tied to this situation."

Both Beatriz and Junie stared at me. I let the silence stretch just a second longer than necessary.

"The Creek Elementary School principal. If the enrollment numbers are the issue, I want to hear what he has to say."

"But, Tony," Junie called as I reached the door, "there are three elementary schools in Apple Creek. How do you know it is that one?"

I smiled over my shoulder.

"Well, only one of them is getting a million-dollar addition."

Chapter 2

There was something about elementary school hallways that always made the day seem brighter. I'd never worked much with young children. Well—never successfully. The only time I'd tried teaching was a four-hour substitute stint right after I joined the district, and it had been a complete disaster. Never again.

Still, since I first started working for the district, my job had involved high school records. I spent hours combing through teenage files—grades, extracurricular activities, college plans, and generations of graduations. I learned far more about the population of Apple Creek than I'd ever expected. Maybe that was why I treasured my occasional visits to the younger students' buildings. They felt... hopeful.

It was probably the colors lining the hallways, the distant laughter drifting in from the playground. Backpacks hung from hooks, art projects spilled cheerfully out of classrooms, and every open door offered a peek into possibility.

And best of all—I wasn't responsible for any of it.

The best part about children is when they're not your problem.

Gertrude seemed to agree. She waddled beside me, head bobbing with purpose, pausing every few steps to inspect a crayon that had escaped into the hallway as though it might be edible. I cleared my throat softly—a signal she occasionally respected—and she flicked her tail feathers before moving on, offended by the implication that she needed guidance.

"Miss Tony?" a voice called. "What brings you here today? I don't believe you're on the agenda."

Anne Sullivan, the school secretary, rose from her chair and walked toward the reception counter.

"Miss Anne," I said, doing my best not to overreact to the alarming amount of paperwork piled behind her—and the file boxes stacked neatly, but suspiciously, in the corner. "I can see you weren't expecting me."

Anne's face turned a shade too close to cherry red, and the quick glance she threw over her shoulder didn't help her case.

That surprised me. Every time I'd visited before, this office had been immaculate. Now it looked like a paper storm had blown through. I wondered if I should start making surprise visits more often—or if something specific had gone wrong here.

"Oh! Yes—well," Anne said, twisting her fingers together. "We had a storage room complication over the weekend. Pipes. Shelves. You know how it goes. We had to pull everything out temporarily. I promise it'll all be back to normal very soon."

I opened my mouth to respond, but a voice I knew far too well floated out of the office just behind the counter.

"I think this should do, Anne. There have to be more incriminating papers in here somewhere."

Penelope Whitcomb emerged carrying a cardboard box that completely obscured her face. She set it down with the others before finally noticing me.

The look of disgust she wore mirrored my own.

"Penelope," I said, crossing my arms. "Why am I not surprised to find you here? Digging up the evidence you promised in your article?"

For a brief, glorious second, she looked caught. Then she recovered, pushing her glasses up her nose.

"It's Penny, Tony. Like I've told you a million times. And I resent your accusation. I'm a professional, and—"

"And only now collecting evidence?" I gestured toward the boxes. "Assuming there's anything useful in them at all. And it's Miss Tony. Like I've told you a million times."

Gertrude chose that moment to quack sharply and peck at a loose corner of one box. Penelope jumped back half a step.

"I have the evidence," Penelope snapped. "And the whistleblower mentioned in my article. The mayor and the city lawyer have already reviewed it. This is simply to clear any remaining doubts—and identify anyone else involved."

Her smile widened, sharp and satisfied. "I just hope your name doesn't come up. Should I prepare for that possibility?"

Experience had taught me not to engage.

As much as I wanted to say something unladylike, I ignored her entirely.

"Miss Anne," I said calmly, "I need to speak with Mr. Hudson. Is he in his office, or should I wait until recess is over?"

Anne hesitated. Penelope's smug expression told me everything before Anne spoke.

"Oh—no, I'm sorry, Miss Tony. Mr. Hudson isn't here. He didn't show up... yet. He might come later. We have the principal-teacher meeting after school."

"Did you know—" I started.

Anne shook her head quickly, and I stopped myself. The last thing we needed was to feed the Gazette another breadcrumb.

"All right, then," I said, forcing a pleasant smile. "I'll come back this afternoon. Please let him know I stopped by."

As I turned toward the door, Gertrude gave one last curious quack and tugged toward the boxes again, as if they'd offended her personally.

Behind me, I heard Penelope laugh.

I didn't look back. I had more important things to do—like finding a missing principal.

Preferably before the reporters did.

The missing principal truly had me worried. I had no doubts about Harold's innocence—not for a second—but Lionel Hudson was still a question mark. I didn't know him well enough to trust my instincts, and the fact that he was nowhere to be found while Whitcomb carted off boxes of files felt like a terrible coincidence.

"Come on, Gertrude," I said as I opened the passenger door of my car. "Let's hope Harold is back at the office so we can get ahead of this."

Gertrude hopped in without ceremony, turned in a tight circle, and settled herself with a disapproving little huff—as if the day had already asked too much of her.

I hadn't even made it out of the parking lot when my phone rang somewhere deep in my purse.

Normally, I wouldn't have answered. I'm a safety-first kind of person. But with Wallace on the other side of the world, I'd learned to make exceptions.

I pulled over and shut off the engine before reaching into the back seat. By the time I fished my phone out, the call had gone to voicemail.

It wasn't Wallace.

It was Harold.

That alone was enough to make my stomach tighten. I called back immediately.

"Tony," Harold said, and the strain in his voice sent a chill straight through me.

"Harold, what's going on?" I asked. "Where are you? We need to clear this up before it gets any worse."

"I know—and—" He paused, breathing hard. "I've been checking the archives, but I can't find what I'm looking for."

"The archives?" I repeated. "Harold, that's on the other side of town. We need you at City Hall. I just came from the elementary school. Mr. Hudson isn't there, and Whitcomb was. You being gone right now doesn't look good."

"I know," he said quietly. "But I've read everything the mayor has. All of it. And it's legitimate."

My grip tightened on the phone.

"There was a fraud, Tony," he continued. "I can't tell you where it started, but it's real. I didn't do it, and I had no idea it was happening—but it's bigger than we thought."

Gertrude shifted in her seat and let out a low, questioning quack, as if she didn't like where this was going either.

"What do you mean, bigger?" I asked.

"The enrollment numbers," Harold said. "Not just at one school. All of them. If the data's been compromised across the district..." He trailed off, then exhaled heavily. "Tony, this might go back years."

My mind raced. The capacity study alone had cost over a million dollars—money approved to expand the elementary school. But if all the schools were affected, then we weren't talking about one bad decision.

We were talking about millions. Possibly more.

"How is that even possible?" I asked.

"That's what I'm trying to figure out," Harold said. "I'm coming back to the office tonight. I need to speak with the mayor and the council as soon as possible. Could you meet me earlier? Around seven?"

"Of course," I said without hesitation.

I trusted Harold completely. If anything, he was too kind for his own good—and people like that were often the easiest to take advantage of.

I glanced at Gertrude, who was now peering intently out the windshield, alert and unusually still.

"We'll be there," I said. "And Harold? We'll figure this out."

After the call ended, Gertrude quacked softly, the kind she saved for moments that mattered.

I hoped she was right.

Because if this went where I feared it might, Junie—and half of Apple Creek—could get pulled under with it.

Chapter 3

I couldn't wait until seven.

The day had already been long enough—trying to piece together what was happening and helping Junie stay calm while we went through boxes and computer files that, to both of us, looked perfectly clear. By five o'clock, I knew sitting still wasn't going to help anyone.

So I drove over to Harold's house.

I didn't know if he'd be home, but logic suggested he might be. Anyone who'd been hauling dusty archive boxes all afternoon and had a meeting with the mayor and council coming up would want time to clean up. At least, that's how my mind worked.

It felt like a win-win.

If Harold was home, I could talk to him

beforehand and get a clearer picture. If he wasn't, maybe Beatriz would be—and if neither of them were there, I could still be back at the office well before seven.

A sensible plan.

Or so I thought.

"I'm not sure Beatriz would appreciate company inside, Gertrude," I said as I opened the passenger door.

My faithful friend hopped down immediately, feathers puffed with confidence. I truly hated how peculiar people could be about ducks. If I'd shown up with a cat or a dog, I wouldn't have to give this speech at all. No wonder Gertrude sometimes behaved a little aggressively around people. She could sense judgment.

"You can enjoy the yard while I check on these people," I added, climbing the porch steps.

That's when I noticed the front door was slightly open.

I stopped.

After years of listening to Wallace talk through cases—what mattered, what didn't, and what never felt right—I knew this wasn't something to ignore. Not necessarily dangerous, but certainly wrong.

I considered calling 911.

Instead, I took a steady breath and went in to take a look.

"Gertrude," I said quietly.

She paused mid-waddle, then swaggered back toward me, settling closer to my ankle. That small, solid presence made me feel a little better. A little safer. I pulled out my phone and dialed Arthur, my son. On any other occasion, I would have called Wallace, but I suppose the medical examiner would do.

"Harold!" I called as I stepped inside the house, waiting for my son to pick up. "Beatriz! The door was open."

I didn't wait for an answer. The house didn't look ransacked, so I figured it wasn't a robbery. Still, my heart thudded as I moved farther in.

"Beatriz!" I called from the bottom of the stairs. If she was upstairs—maybe in the shower—she might not hear me, and the last thing I wanted was to scare her half to death.

"Mom," Arthur's voice suddenly filled my ear, making me jump. "I promise I'll stop at the store later, but I'm still at work and—"

"Arthur," I cut in. "I think there's someone in Harold's house."

"What are you—who is Harold? Where are you?"

Too many questions, too fast, and his sharp tone didn't help my nerves at all.

"Well, Harold Wilkins is our superintendent and my boss," I snapped quietly. "For many years now. You should know that, Arthur."

I heard him say something else, but my mind didn't register it. I'd turned toward the office.

That's when I saw Harold.

"Tony... I didn't—I don't know—he was like this when—"

Gertrude suddenly quacked—loud and indignant—and rushed past me, wings flapping as she barreled straight into the room. She bumped into Harold's legs with surprising force, driving him backward.

In my ear, Arthur's voice grew urgent, but my eyes were locked on the figure lying on the carpet in front of the dark wooden desk.

Harold stumbled back, and when the knife clattered to the floor, I finally noticed the blood on his hands.

My silly mind latched onto one useless thought: how expensive it would be to clean the carpet. If it could even be cleaned at all.

That absurd detail snapped me fully back into the moment.

"Mom! Are you there? Mom!"

"I'm here," I said, forcing my voice to stay calm.

I'd heard plenty about crime over the years, and dinner conversations with my medical examiner son could be... vivid. But this was the first time I'd ever found a body.

And possibly the person who killed him.

"Arthur," I said carefully, watching Harold's trembling hands, "I think we're going to need the police."

If Harold was a killer, he was doing a poor job of looking like one. He looked panicked, not dangerous. When he nodded weakly and stepped back again, I knew it in my bones.

He was innocent.

"The police?" Arthur repeated sharply. "Mom!"

"Well," I said, glancing at the still figure on the floor as Gertrude stood protectively between me and Harold, feathers fluffed to twice her size, "an ambulance would be a waste."

"The man is dead."

I was sitting by the kitchen counter, waiting for the police to take my statement, with Gertrude pressed against my leg.

Although I should have known better, I was still surprised when Arthur showed up at the house. He came in with the first patrol car and walked straight toward me. My sweet boy wrapped me in a hug as if I'd been in an accident and then—barely two seconds later—started scolding me for being irresponsible and not waiting outside for the police.

If he hadn't looked so genuinely worried, I would have stopped his rant immediately. That was no way to talk to his mother, and he knew better. Still, I couldn't deny the sense of comfort that came with it.

It wasn't so terrible to have someone worry about you once in a while.

While Arthur paced and talked, I let my eyes drift around the kitchen.

It looked exactly like the kitchens I'd seen all over this part of Apple Creek—probably even like my own, if I were being honest. The same dependable refrigerator model, the same slightly outdated stove, a coffee maker that had seen better mornings but still did its job. Clean counters, sensible cabinets, nothing fancy and nothing neglected.

I'd never been inside Harold's house before, but this was precisely what I would have expected to find.

And yet.

I rested my hand on Gertrude's back as she shifted beside me. She studied the room with serious intent, head cocked, then gave a soft, uncertain quack and nudged the edge of the counter with her bill.

"I know," I murmured to her. "Something is off."

"Something is off?" Arthur asked as he turned back to me, clearly annoyed. "Of course there is something off, Mom. There is a body down the hallway! You—" He shook his head, throwing his arms up. "I can't even—" He turned and walked out of the room.

He could be right.

But somehow, I knew it was something else.

Then an officer entered the kitchen, and just like that, Harold was handcuffed and led away. The brief glimpse I caught of his face—pale, shaken, completely lost—settled heavily in my chest.

All my thoughts were replaced by an image of poor Harold sitting alone in a cell at the station.

I worried about him. I didn't doubt his innocence—not for a moment—but there were too many things stacked against him. Being found alone with the body and the murder weapon was bad enough. The fraud investigation only added fuel to the fire, turning suspicion into something that looked dangerously like motive.

And Harold hadn't given me much to work with beyond a shaken, heartfelt *I didn't do it.*

Shock does that to people.

Gertrude wandered the length of the kitchen, her steps quick and restless. I didn't blame her. Patrol officers moved in and out of the room, radios crackling, boots thudding against the tile. The last thing I needed was Gertrude deciding to defend her territory and chasing a uniformed officer across a crime scene.

I was just about to ask if I could take her outside when raised voices echoed through the house.

"What do you mean you can't let me in?" a sharp voice snapped from the front hall. "This is a public matter. People deserve answers. Who is in charge here?"

I froze.

Gertrude did too.

"Oh no," I muttered under my breath.

Arthur reappeared in the doorway just as quickly, his expression tightening. "That would be her," he said.

From the office, a young woman with a gentle face and long hair pulled back into a ponytail stepped forward.

"I'm Detective Patricia Green," her voice cut through the tension—calm, controlled, and just firm enough to carry. "And Miss Whitcomb, this is an active crime scene. You need to step outside."

"I'm a member of the press," Penny replied, her tone smooth but insistent. "The public has a right to know what's happening in their own community."

"The public will be informed when appropriate," Detective Green said. "Right now, you're interfering with an investigation."

There was a pause—just long enough to suggest Penny was deciding how far she could push.

Then:

"I already know a superintendent has been detained," she said. "And a principal is dead. I'd say the public would consider that appropriate."

Arthur swore under his breath.

Detective Green didn't raise her voice.

"Officer," she said, without looking away from Penny, "please escort Miss Whitcomb outside."

"Yes, ma'am."

There was the sound of movement, a brief protest—

"This isn't over," Penny added sharply, her voice already retreating toward the door. "People will hear about this."

"I'm counting on it," Detective Green replied.

The front door shut.

Silence settled over the house again, though it felt different now—less contained, somehow.

Like whatever had happened here was already slipping beyond these walls.

Arthur let out a slow breath. "That's going to be all over the Gazette by morning."

"Worse," I said quietly. "She has an evening section."

And I had no doubt it wouldn't sound anything like the truth.

Before I could say more, another voice rose from deeper inside the house.

"What are you talking about?" Beatriz

shouted, her voice high and frantic. “Where is Harold? I need to see him!”

I moved toward the doorway in time to see an officer trying—politely but unsuccessfully—to block her path. Detective Green once again, walked out of the office.

“Mrs. Wilkins, I presume,” she said, her voice calm but firm.

Beatriz stopped struggling and looked the woman up and down. “And you are?”

“I’m the detective in charge of the investigation.”

“What investigation? Where is Harold? Is he—” Beatriz clapped a hand over her mouth as tears spilled free.

The officer reached out to steady her, and I hurried forward, placing a hand on her shoulder.

“It’s all right, Beatriz,” I said softly. “Harold isn’t dead.”

She looked at me in shock, then threw her arms around me. “Thank goodness. Then what is going—”

“Mrs. Wilkins,” Detective Green interrupted gently. “I need to ask you a few questions. Please come with me.”

Her tone left no room for argument. I met Beatriz’s eyes and gave her a small, encouraging nod as she followed the detective down the hallway.

The last thing I heard was a sharp cry from Beatriz—raw and heartbroken—as she reached the office and finally saw what waited there.

Principal Found Dead Amid Ongoing School District Investigation

By Penelope "Penny" Whitcomb
Apple Creek Gazette

APPLE CREEK — The quiet town of Apple Creek was shaken Wednesday evening when Lionel Hudson, principal of Creek Elementary School, was found dead inside a private residence under circumstances authorities have confirmed are suspicious.

Police responded to the home of Superintendent Harold P. Wilkins shortly after 5:00 p.m. Following an initial assessment of the scene, Wilkins was taken into custody for questioning. Officials have not yet confirmed whether formal charges will be filed.

The death comes less than forty eight hours

after the Gazette reported concerns surrounding missing funds tied to a district-commissioned enrollment and capacity study. That investigation, which already raised questions about financial oversight and data accuracy, now appears to be connected to a far more serious situation.

Sources close to the case indicate that Mr. Hudson may have had access to enrollment records currently under review. Whether his role was administrative, investigative, or otherwise remains unclear.

Authorities have released few details, but Detective Patricia Green, who is leading the investigation, stated that "all possibilities remain under consideration" and urged the public to avoid speculation.

Despite that request, speculation has already begun—and in some corners of the community, it has escalated into outright outrage.

Parents gathered outside Creek Elementary School demanding immediate answers from district officials. Several described the situation as "deeply troubling," while others questioned how a financial investigation could spiral into what appears to be a violent crime.

"There's more going on here than they're telling us," said one parent, who declined to be named. "First the missing money, and now a death? That's not a coincidence."

Unconfirmed reports suggest that multiple families are reconsidering their children's enrollment for the upcoming school year, citing concerns over safety and transparency within the district.

While no official statements support these claims, the growing unease throughout Apple Creek is difficult to ignore.

At this time, it remains unknown whether the financial investigation and Mr. Hudson's death are directly linked.

The School District has not issued a public statement to what some residents are calling the most serious scandal Apple Creek has faced in decades.

As the situation continues to develop, the Gazette will provide updates as more information becomes available.

Chapter 4

Then it was my turn.

I'd already rummaged through the refrigerator and found something suitable for Gertrude—frozen peas. She accepted them with impressive dignity, which lasted exactly three seconds before she demanded more, quacking sharply as Arthur appeared in the kitchen doorway.

"Mom," he said, rubbing the back of his neck, "I want you to meet someone."

Now, as the mother of a grown man who'd had his heart broken more than once—and never gently—that sentence alone was enough to put me on edge.

I turned slowly.

"Detective Green," I said, not bothering to

soften my tone. "I presume it's my turn to answer questions."

Arthur's face took on the familiar look of a long-suffering martyr, but I ignored it. Gertrude did not. She paused mid-pea, lifted her head, and fixed the detective with one bright, unblinking eye.

"I know you've been waiting a while," Detective Green said. "And I appreciate your patience."

Her smile was genuine. That was the unsettling part.

I didn't trust her, and I knew exactly why.

First, she wasn't from Apple Creek. I worked for the school district, and while my desk didn't see everyone, it saw enough names that I noticed when one never appeared. Second, she'd just had a good friend of mine arrested—a man I believed, without hesitation, was innocent. And third—yes, this might sound petty—she spoke with a softness that suggested she already knew how people would react to her.

I didn't like that feeling at all.

"Then let's get on with it," I said, folding my arms. "I'd like to go home."

"Mom," Arthur warned quietly.

"It's all right," Detective Green said,

holding up a hand without even looking at him. "I've found your mother prefers efficiency."

That earned her a point she hadn't asked for—and cost her my goodwill.

Gertrude let out a low, suspicious quack and edged closer to my leg.

Detective Green noticed. Of course she did.

"I like your duck," she added pleasantly. "She seems... perceptive."

"She is," I said. "And she bites when she doesn't like someone."

Gertrude puffed her feathers, just enough to make the point.

The detective's smile didn't falter. If anything, it warmed. "Fair enough."

She turned back to me. "Why don't you walk me through what you saw?"

I sighed and did exactly that. From the moment I arrived to the moment the officers took over, I laid it all out—clear, careful, and complete. I made sure to be thorough. I had no intention of answering the same questions twice.

When I finished, she glanced down at her notes and said, "The front door was open. Correct?"

I nodded. "Yes. I've never been inside this

house before. Why would I come through the back?"

Her eyes flicked up at that—not surprised, just attentive. She tapped her pencil once against her lip.

"And you didn't see anyone leaving?" she asked. "On foot, or by car?"

That was... smart.

If Harold had come upon the scene afterward, why leave the door open? And if Lionel had arrived on his own, why leave it that way unless he planned to leave quickly—which didn't fit with how things ended.

No. An open door suggested interruption.

Someone else leaving in a hurry.

I shook my head. "No. I didn't see anyone."

Gertrude let out a thoughtful quack, the kind she saved for moments when she seemed to agree with me more than she understood why.

Detective Green watched us both, her expression soft but sharp underneath.

"Thank you," she said. "That helps."

A small, unwilling smirk tugged at my mouth.

I still didn't like her.

But I was beginning to think she might actually be good at her job.

And that, I had to admit, was very good news for Harold.

Although part of me wanted to go straight to the station and talk to Harold, there was no point in it. I wasn't family, and there was little to no chance Chief Ben would allow me anywhere near him.

Instead, I went back to the district department, just as planned.

By the time I arrived, word had already spread through Apple Creek. Everyone seemed to know what had happened, and the meeting with the council had been canceled. That suited me just fine. It gave me time to do some digging of my own into this fraud mess.

I expected the office to be empty. It was late, and those of us in the school district prided ourselves on efficiency. We didn't need extra hours to keep things running.

So when I saw the lights on—and Harold's office door standing open—I felt a flicker of panic.

I suppose finding a body earlier in the day will do that to you.

"Who's there?" I called as I stepped cautiously inside.

"Tony! It's you!" Junie burst out of the office, relief flooding her face. "Thank goodness you came back. I need your help. They're going to blame me!"

I set my purse down on her desk and moved past her toward the office. It had finally sunk in what the fraud accusation could do to her—and the murder certainly hadn't helped matters. I was about to say something when I stopped short in the doorway.

Files and papers were scattered across the floor of Harold's office, covering nearly every available surface. This hadn't been a quick search. This was hours of work. At least Junie had a solid alibi for the larger crime.

"What's all this?" I asked, taking it in.

Junie ran both hands through her hair and looked around, her expression pure panic.

"I swear, Tony, none of this was here last week when Harold and I reviewed the new enrollments."

That was not what I wanted to hear.

"What do you mean?" I asked carefully. "What did you find?"

"Extra files," she said, pointing toward the

computer on her desk. "But they're fake. Missing information. After you left, I started gathering everything we might need for an audit. That's when I noticed new entries in the system."

She swallowed hard. "That shouldn't be possible. I didn't enter them—and every time there's a new enrollment, I get a notification because I have to authorize it."

She bit her lip, her hands tangling in her hair again. "I thought maybe it was a hack. So I came in to match the system with the paperwork the schools send us. When I checked the Creek Elementary School files, I found fake students—matching the entries exactly."

Junie began pacing, careful not to step on anything.

"I had to keep looking, and every school is the same," she continued. "Tony, all of them have fake student files. I didn't do this. And how could they have my signature? You know me. I would never—"

"I know, sweetheart," I said gently.

I crouched down and picked up one of the elementary school folders. It felt shockingly thin, and when I opened it, there was no question it was missing everything but the enrollment form. Guardian authorization, liability waivers, sports acknowledgments, medical and emergency contacts—all of it gone.

Junie's signature and Harold's approval were there.

"When was the last time you checked these?" I asked.

Junie paused, thinking. "Friday, I think. We updated the new enrollments and filed them before the weekend." Her voice cracked. "Tony, what am I going to do?"

Right on cue, Detective Green appeared in the doorway, accompanied by a uniformed officer.

"Mrs. Cooper," she said calmly. "I wasn't expecting to find you here."

I straightened and crossed my arms. "And why not? This is my office. And thanks to you, I've already lost most of my workday."

Her eyes flicked briefly around the room—just long enough to tell me she was cataloging everything—before she turned to Junie.

"Mrs. McCarthy?"

Junie nodded, her fear unmistakable.

"I need you to come down to the station with me," Detective Green said gently. "There are a few questions we need you to answer."

"Why can't you ask them here?" I

snapped. "She hasn't done anything wrong. And as you can see, she's been here all day. There's no way she could have murdered Lionel."

"Murder?" Junie gasped, staring at me.

Only then did I realize she'd been too busy to catch up on Apple Creek gossip—a rare oversight on her part.

Detective Green glanced from Junie to me, then leaned toward the officer and murmured something I couldn't hear. He nodded and stepped out of the office.

"If you'd prefer to answer questions here, Mrs. McCarthy, I have no objection," the detective said.

I felt a small surge of victory—until she turned to me.

"However," she continued, "this is a police investigation. I can't have you present during an interrogation."

I frowned, my thoughts racing.

If I stayed, I could keep an eye on the files.

If Junie were taken down to the police department, she'd be terrified.

I looked at her. The silent plea in her eyes decided it.

"I'll leave you to it," I said.

As I passed Detective Green, I stopped and

met her gaze. "But make no mistake—I'm watching this investigation closely."

She didn't flinch. In fact, she smiled.

"I wouldn't expect anything else, Miss Tony."

And that, somehow, unsettled me more than if she'd bristled.

School District Employee Questioned as Fraud Investigation Deepens
By Penelope "Penny" Whitcomb
Apple Creek Gazette

APPLE CREEK — The investigation into missing school district funds took a significant turn late Wednesday as authorities confirmed that a district employee has been formally questioned in connection with both the financial discrepancies and the death of Creek Elementary School principal Lionel Hudson.

Junie McCarthy, a long-time records coordinator with the Apple Creek School District, was brought in for questioning following the discovery of irregularities in enrollment documentation tied to multiple schools.

While police have not announced any formal charges, sources indicate that McCarthy's role in maintaining and authorizing student records has placed her at the center of the ongoing investigation.

Detective Patricia Green declined to comment on specific individuals but confirmed that "persons with direct access to enrollment data are a key focus of the inquiry."

The development has left many in the community stunned.

McCarthy, who has worked in the district for over a decade, was widely regarded as a dependable and familiar presence within the department. However, some residents now question whether that long-standing access may have provided the opportunity for misconduct.

"It's always the ones you don't expect," said one resident, who asked not to be identified. "She would have known exactly how to make changes without anyone noticing."

Others expressed concern over the possibility that the fraud investigation—and Mr. Hudson's death—may be more closely connected than previously believed.

"If the records were manipulated," another parent commented, "then whoever did it had a reason. And now someone is dead." A few residents have expressed concern about how closely McCarthy worked with Superintendent Wilkins, raising questions about whether others in the department may also face scrutiny.

Unconfirmed reports suggest that additional discrepancies have been discovered across multiple schools, raising questions about how long the issue may have gone unnoticed—and who else might be involved.

Despite growing speculation, officials have urged the public to remain patient as the investigation continues.

Still, tensions appear to be rising.

Several parents contacted by the Gazette described feeling "uneasy" about the situation, with some calling for immediate administrative changes within the district while the investigation is ongoing.

While no official statement has confirmed McCarthy's involvement in any wrongdoing, her connection to the records under review has made her a person of interest in what is quickly becoming one of the most complex cases Apple Creek has faced in recent years.

As the investigation unfolds, the Gazette will continue to follow developments closely.

Chapter 5

"Mom," Arthur said as he walked into the kitchen the next morning. "You could have been nicer to Tricia. She's under a lot of pressure with this investigation, and the last thing she needs is your judgment."

I ignored him at first.

This was my house, and he had no right to come in here and correct my behavior—or my personality. I opened the back door for Gertrude, who immediately squawked and flapped her wings as she waddled out onto the deck, thrilled by the morning air.

I wrapped both hands around my coffee mug and took a breath, keeping my voice even.

"She must not be a very good detective if a single murder puts that much pressure on her."

As expected, my son snapped.

"She is a good detective," he said sharply. "Or she'll prove it with this case. And no detective needs your input on a crime, Mom. Not even Dad."

Of course he brought up his father.

What Arthur didn't realize—or perhaps chose to forget—was that Wallace talked to me about his cases all the time. He never shared confidential details, but he trusted my instincts. More than once, a casual observation of mine had sent him looking in a new direction.

I might not have worn a badge, but I knew how investigations worked.

Rather than argue, I circled back to the part that mattered.

"What does she need to prove?" I asked. "I don't recall you ever saying your other troublemaker friend had to prove himself."

Arthur groaned. "Logan is not a troublemaker. He's been on the job for years. Tricia just got promoted two months ago, and this case is a big one." He looked at me squarely. "I'm asking you—please don't interfere with her investigation."

I walked to the sink, setting my mug down more carefully than necessary. I didn't want to upset him. I just didn't like this detective—or the way Arthur said her name.

And I couldn't tell whether that unease came from the fact that the case involved my friends... or from something older and more maternal that I didn't care to examine too closely.

"Why would Ben put someone so new on a murder case?" I asked. "Does he think it's not important? Or does he think it's already solved? Harold stabbed Lionel. Case closed."

"That's not true, Mom," Arthur said firmly. "You know Chief Ben wouldn't close a case like that. Tricia is investigating what happened. She needs the forensics. She's talking to everyone involved in the fraud."

I waved a hand dismissively. "She can't be that good if she needs forensics. Even I know Lionel was stabbed in the back with the knife found beside him."

I chuckled. "If she needs your report to figure that out, then she isn't—"

"If the knife had been the primary cause of death," Arthur interrupted, his voice suddenly measured, "there would have been active bleeding consistent with a functioning heart."

I froze.

"If it had been that simple," he continued,

eyes fixed on the table, "the stab would've happened while his heart was working the way it should. There would've been a lot more blood. No signs of a struggle. No defensive wounds." He shook his head. "His skin tone, Mom... this wasn't sudden trauma followed by death. His heart was already failing—or had already failed —when the knife went in."

Silence settled between us.

"No," he said abruptly, standing up. "I'm not talking to you about this. You did that on purpose."

I lifted my shoulders and smiled faintly. "I didn't do anything, Arthur. We've talked about your cases plenty of times before. I don't see how this one is different."

He narrowed his eyes, grabbed his coat, and headed for the door. I followed him.

"So that means Harold couldn't be the killer," I said quickly. "And if Lionel's heart failed first, then what caused it? Do you know—"

Arthur turned, pointing a finger at me.

"No, Mom. I'm not discussing this. Stay out of it." His voice softened just a touch. "This isn't a game. Someone is dead. And there are people out there who loved him. Think about that."

The door shut behind him with a solid thud.

Gertrude came scrambling back inside, quacking indignantly as if she'd missed something important.

"You're right," I said, crouching to rub her feathers. "He does have a point."

Gertrude tilted her head.

"We should think about who's missing Lionel," I added quietly.

And why.

For the first time all year, I arrived at the department before Junie.

Under normal circumstances, I would have made a fuss about it. Today, it only made me uneasy.

I used the quiet to check Harold's office. Seeing yellow crime scene tape stretched across the doorway stopped me short. That unsettled me more than I expected. The only people in the department last night had been Junie and Detective Green. I probably should have stayed and gone through the papers while I had the chance—but there was no use regretting it now.

Instead, I sat down at Junie's desk.

The files stacked there were ordinary—routine paperwork, nothing suspicious at first glance. As far as I could tell, there was nothing that explained how those enrollment records had appeared out of nowhere. Junie was right: if it had been a hack, it could have been done remotely. But hacking and paper records meant something else entirely.

Someone inside the department.

I didn't like that thought at all.

"Miss Tony."

The now-familiar gentle voice from the doorway made my stomach tighten.

"Mrs. McCarthy said you'd arrive early," Detective Green continued. "May I speak with you?"

Gertrude, who had been waddling under Junie's desk investigating a forgotten paperclip, emerged at once. She took one look at the detective and—without hesitation—ambled straight toward her.

Well.

That was new.

Gertrude circled Detective Green's shoes once, then settled calmly near her feet, looking up with mild interest instead of suspicion.

I frowned. "You usually don't do that."

Detective Green smiled, clearly amused but careful not to move. "I'll take that as a compliment."

"I wouldn't," I said dryly, though I made a mental note of it.

I stayed seated and crossed my arms. "Where is Junie?"

Her expression softened—not alarmed, just concerned.

"You arrested her last night and closed my department as a crime scene," I continued before she could answer. "How dare you? You have no proof she was involved in the murder, and I'm certain Harold is innocent as well."

She sighed and paced the length of the office once before replying.

"I had to close Mr. Wilkins's office because of the evidence inside. We can't risk losing anything that might prove—or disprove—the guilt of the suspects."

I opened my mouth to argue, but she raised her hands gently.

"We haven't met properly," she said, "but I know who you are. Arthur spoke highly of you. So did Maggie Willow."

That gave me pause.

I liked Maggie. She had always treated Gertrude like she belonged here—which mattered more than people realized—and she was sharp. I'd helped her just last fall when she untangled that mess at the Historical Farm. Using her as a reference was... smart.

Very smart.

"I had to arrest Mr. Wilkins," she went on, lowering her voice as she sat across from me. "But I agree with you. I don't believe he committed the murder. And I don't believe Mrs. McCarthy committed the fraud."

That wasn't what I expected.

"I do need to understand how the fraud happened," she added, "if neither of them were involved. And I don't have much to work with. That's why I'm here."

Before I could respond, the office door opened.

Beatriz stepped inside—and stopped short when she saw us.

"Oh. I'm sorry," she said. "I didn't mean to interrupt. I just need to grab a few personal things from Harold's office."

Detective Green stood immediately. "I'm afraid I can't allow that. The office is part of an active investigation."

Beatriz's jaw tightened. "You've already taken my husband. Now you're taking his things?"

"What exactly do you need?" the detective asked calmly. "You mentioned before that your consulting work with the district ended weeks ago."

"That has nothing to do with this," Beatriz snapped, then caught herself. She took a breath. "Harold spent more time in that office than he did at home. He brought half his life with him. His jacket, his mug, and his plants."

I blinked. "His plants?"

"Yes," she said, nodding toward the taped doorway. "The fern by the window and the little jade on the shelf. He watered them every Friday. If no one does it, they'll die."

It sounded so... ordinary. So Harold.

Detective Green hesitated—just a moment.

"I understand the concern," she said. "But I can't let anyone enter the office. Anything inside will remain secured until the investigation is closed."

Beatriz opened her mouth to argue, then stopped. Her shoulders sagged instead.

"At least tell me someone will water them," she said quietly. "They didn't do anything wrong."

That landed harder than any accusation.

Detective Green glanced at the taped door, then back at Beatriz. "I'll make a note of it."

Gertrude gave a soft, agreeable quack, as if seconding the idea.

The detective turned back to me and handed me a business card. "If you're willing to sit down with me and talk through the fraud, I'd appreciate it. Just let me know what works for you."

And then she left.

I stood there with more questions than answers—and Beatriz unraveling beside me.

Which told me one thing for certain.

This investigation was already far more complicated than it looked.

Chapter 6

Beatriz stared at me for a long second after Detective Green left the office. Then her face crumpled, and she stepped forward, folding into me as if she'd run out of strength altogether.

"I don't know what to do, Tony," she said, her voice breaking. "Harold is devastated. And what the lawyer says... it isn't good."

I rested a hand on the back of her head.

"All of this will clear up," I said, slipping into that steady, maternal tone I kept for moments like this. "Harold didn't do anything wrong. The police will figure that out."

Beatriz pulled back just enough to look at me.

"Are you certain he didn't have anything to do with the fraud?"

The question landed heavier than she probably intended. Her eyes were shiny, uncertain—full of questions she wanted someone else to answer for her.

"You doubt him?" I asked gently.

She shook her head and paced the length of the office, her heels clicking sharply against the floor. Gertrude, who had been minding her own business near the window, lifted her head and watched with interest.

"No," Beatriz said at last. "I don't doubt that he didn't hurt the principal, but—" She bit her lip and lowered her voice. "He's been acting strange these last two weeks, Tony. When I asked him about it, he just waved me off."

She gestured vaguely toward the stacks of folders. "It must have been the workload, right?"

That was the problem.

In the school district, there were times of the year when the pressure was relentless—end of term, the start of a new school year, graduation deadlines, credential checks, parent board meetings stacked one on top of the other.

But this wasn't one of those times.

We were squarely in the middle of the year.

Even my desk was manageable. Harold's should have been too.

I didn't like the implication forming in my mind. What I liked even less was that Beatriz should have known that.

They'd been married a long time.

"How strange?" I asked.

She stopped pacing and let her arms fall to her sides. "I don't know. On edge. Distracted." She searched my face. "You must have noticed it too, Tony, haven't you?"

"I'm not sure," I said honestly.

Beatriz looked down at the floor, then gave a small, brittle smile. "You're probably right. I'm reading into things." She glanced around the office again, as if seeing it for the first time. "I don't even know why I'm here. Since when do I care about plants and office arrangements?" She gave a short laugh. "I just need... answers."

At that moment, Gertrude chose to waddle over and peck decisively at the hem of Beatriz's skirt.

Beatriz startled, then laughed—for real this time. "Oh—hello there."

Gertrude quacked once.

"Careful," I said. "She's very protective of greenery."

That, at least, earned a smile.

"I understand," I said, touching Beatriz's shoulder and waiting until she looked at me again. "We all need answers."

My phone rang before she could respond.

"Tony!" Junie's voice came through loud and urgent. "I need your help. Now."

I glanced at Beatriz—at her tear-streaked face—and felt a tightening in my chest.

"Be right there," I said into the phone.

Before leaving the office, I gave everyone the rest of the day off and locked the department behind me. I didn't like Detective Green going through my people's work any more than I liked strangers rearranging my kitchen drawers—but she was right. If there was something buried in those piles of paper, it was better they stayed untouched.

I walked Beatriz out, then drove straight to Junie's house.

I had been expecting reporters clustered on the sidewalk, maybe a patrol car parked at the curb, officers ready to escort her away. Instead, Junie was alone on her porch, waving both arms like she was trying to flag down a rescue helicopter.

She hurried toward the car the second I pulled into the driveway.

"Thank goodness, Tony," she said, opening the car door without hesitation. "I can't stay at home another minute or I may commit a murder."

Gertrude quacked sharply from the front passenger seat, clearly offended by the competition.

Junie groaned but closed the door and climbed into the back seat. "Bob should be in charge of the case. He thinks he knows everything."

"Maybe he knows—"

"He doesn't, Tony!" she snapped. "He didn't even know who Harold was until he heard the news last night, and had no idea Harold was my boss until I told him he might want to talk to the police. And then—" she waved a hand dramatically—"he turned into a conspiracy expert with theories no one asked for and facts he made up himself."

I chuckled, not for the first time wondering how they'd stayed married all these years. Retirement hadn't helped their harmony much, but then again, it had never been all roses and chocolates over there. There was a reason both of Junie's children lived in Stonefield Shore and visited sparingly.

"Sometimes conspiracies aren't entirely useless, Junie," I said. "They give you a starting point. For example—what do you know about Lionel, besides the fact that he was the elementary school principal of a school tied to a fraud investigation?"

Of course, I didn't know more than that, but I was counting on my friend's town knowledge. In the rearview mirror, I saw her frown as she considered it.

"Well," she said slowly, "he's been divorced for a few years. No kids that I know of. He played golf with Bob a handful of times." She lowered her voice. "And rumor had it he was quite the catch among the teachers. Might've been the reason for the divorce, if you know what I mean."

That was interesting.

"There aren't many stronger motives than jealousy," I murmured. "Do you know who the other party in the affair might have been?"

"No, Tony," she said. After a brief moment, she lowered her voice and added, "Now, this might be nothing, but last month—during the Parents' Board appreciation meeting—Rita

Carver was very upset with a first-grade teacher. Marina Lopez, I think."

I frowned. "A month ago? When did Lionel get divorced?"

"I couldn't tell you," Junie said. "But both women were furious, and neither of them was Lionel's ex-wife."

I glanced at her. "You're saying there may have been more than one affair."

"I can't tell, but—this part only stuck with me later—about two weeks ago Harold was asking questions about transferring a teacher midyear. Which is odd, isn't it?"

The light turned red, and I turned to look at her fully. "Rita wanted this teacher out of the elementary school?"

Junie lifted her shoulder. "Not sure, but Harold started asking about a midterm transfer for Miss Lopez."

"And did he transfer her?"

"No," Junie said. "She quit."

The car behind me honked impatiently. I turned back to the road, resisting the very strong urge to open the window and let Gertrude express her opinion on public manners.

Gertrude, of course, quacked at the car.

"Let's go to the school," I said, changing

direction. "Marina Lopez may be gone, but Anne will know something."

Junie nodded, leaned back—then immediately leaned forward again. "Do you think Rita Carver could've started the enrollment fraud to get back at Harold?"

A light switched on in my mind.

I'd been thinking about the motive for the murder. But Junie was right—revenge like that didn't have to stop with Lionel. As president of the Parents' Board, Rita Carver had influence, access, and more reason than most to want Harold embarrassed.

Gertrude quacked softly, as if she agreed.

Chapter 7

Junie and I were luckier than I'd expected.

I had braced myself for Anne Sullivan to be defensive—tight-lipped, nervous, unwilling to talk to either of us. Especially Junie. By now, there couldn't be a soul in Apple Creek who hadn't heard her name whispered alongside the word *fraud*.

Instead, the moment we stepped into the elementary school office, we walked straight into a storm.

"I don't care about your supposed rules," Rita Carver was shouting, her face far too close to Anne's. "As a parent, this is unacceptable. And as president of the Parents' Board, I will get answers for the families of this school."

Anne looked pale but held her ground. "I

can't release school files without permission from the principal or the superintendent. You know that, Rita."

Rita stepped closer. Too close.

"Well, the principal is dead and the superintendent is in jail," she snapped. "So who exactly do you suggest I talk to, Anne?"

Anne opened her mouth to answer—and then saw me standing in the doorway.

Relief crossed her face like sunlight after a storm.

"Miss Tony," she said quickly. "Could you help me, please?"

Gertrude chose that moment to waddle past my feet and give a curious quack, her feet clicking against the tile like punctuation.

Rita turned.

The instant she saw me, she straightened, crossed her arms, and pulled her shoulders back. We'd crossed paths before. Those encounters had never ended in her favor.

I didn't care for people who abused their titles, and Rita Carver treated hers like a weapon.

"What seems to be the problem?" I asked, my voice calm—but firm.

"Well," Anne began—

"I need to see the school's enrollment files,"

Rita cut in. "If there's anything being hidden, the families deserve to know. And with Li—Mr. Hudson gone, someone needs to make sure of that."

The stumble over Lionel's name didn't escape me.

I nodded slowly and mirrored her stance, folding my arms. "And you believe that someone should be you?"

"I'm more than qualified to—"

"How exactly are you qualified to take over a principal's role?" I asked.

She opened her mouth, but this time I didn't let her speak.

"You don't have an educational degree or any background as a teacher," I said evenly. "According to the biography you submitted to the Parents' Board—the one you used during the election—you studied marketing and business but never worked in the field. You chose instead to focus on what you described as ensuring a quality educational program for Apple Creek's children. Is that correct?"

I paused, then added quietly,

"Or did you lie to win your position on the board?"

Anne gasped and covered her mouth.

Junie, on the other hand, sat down and made herself comfortable.

If there was one thing people in Apple Creek knew—or should have known—about me, it was that I spoke my mind. I didn't soften the truth just to spare someone's feelings.

"I did not lie to win the board election, Tony," Rita said sharply. "I care about the well-being of the students and their families—"

Her voice cracked at the end of the sentence.

"I've heard you," I said. "But demanding confidential files while the police are investigating both fraud and murder doesn't make you look concerned. It makes you look impatient."

I paused.

"Or nervous."

Something flickered across her face.

"Why do you want to see those files, Rita?" I asked quietly. "You wouldn't know what to look for unless you already suspected something. And if that's the case, perhaps the police should be involved."

"I don't know anything more than—"

"Where were you yesterday morning?" I asked.

The words cut cleanly through the room.

"When Lionel Hudson was killed."

She froze.

"I—I was at home," she said. "Working."

"At home, or working?" I asked gently. "Those aren't always the same thing."

"I work from home!"

The answer came too fast.

"Very convenient," I said. "Can anyone verify that?"

Gertrude chose that moment to flap her wings once, sharply, as if even she sensed the tension.

Rita shook her head, words tangling as she tried to respond, so I pressed on—perhaps a touch too quickly.

"You had a relationship with Lionel," I said. "You were involved with him after his divorce, and then you became jealous when he started seeing one of the teachers, Marina Lopez. So you decided to take matters into your own hands. Is that right?"

"Stop it!" Rita snapped.

The force of it surprised even her.

She backed away until she hit the wall, her hands lifting as though she could push the accusation away.

"I didn't—Miss Lopez—" Her voice faltered.

I'll admit it—I was enjoying myself a little too much.

"So you're denying you wanted Miss Lopez removed from the school," I continued, "because of a personal vendetta?"

"I didn't—"

She stopped.

Closed her eyes.

Took a long, slow breath that seemed to scrape its way out of her chest.

When she looked at me again, the anger had drained out of her face.

What remained looked dangerously close to collapse.

"Yes," she said quietly. "Lionel and I were in a relationship. Or at least... I thought we were."

Her gaze dropped to the floor.

"It was after his divorce. I'd heard the rumors about his behavior while he was married, but I didn't believe them until—"

Her fingers twisted together.

"Until I found the note."

She swallowed.

"He'd written it to Marina. About how wonderful their dinner had been. How much he was looking forward to seeing her again. Asking if she liked the flowers."

Junie and Anne stood behind me, silent now, and I could feel the weight of Rita's words settle over all of us.

There was no doubt she had loved Lionel —whatever form that love had taken.

And I began to wonder if the anger I'd seen earlier hadn't been fury at all, but grief with nowhere safe to land.

"What was I supposed to do?" Rita asked, her voice breaking. "Marina is at least fifteen years younger than me."

She laughed weakly, though there was no humor in it.

"I know it was wrong, but I was so angry. Angry at her—yes—but mostly at myself."

Her hand pressed against her chest.

"I felt ashamed. Like a complete fool."

Gertrude, who had been lingering near the doorway, waddled closer and sat down a few feet from Rita, her head tilted, dark eyes fixed on her face.

She didn't quack.

She didn't move.

She just watched.

Rita didn't seem to notice. Or maybe she didn't care anymore.

"After I spoke to Harold..." She gave a small, embarrassed smile. "He was kind to me.

Kinder than I deserved, probably. He talked me out of doing something I would have regretted."

Her smile faded.

"I swear, I don't know why Marina quit. As far as I know, Harold was only going to warn Lionel—tell him to stop involving teachers in his personal mess."

She swallowed hard.

"And I didn't speak to Lionel after that. Not after I threw his things out. Not after I broke everything that reminded me of him."

Gertrude shifted closer, settling against Rita's shoe, warm and solid.

Rita glanced down, startled.

Then she reached out without thinking, resting her fingers lightly on Gertrude's back.

"You must have noticed," Rita said quietly, looking back at us. "How I stopped coming here. I stopped visiting Lionel once I understood what he'd done."

Her voice wavered.

"And now he's gone."

The tears came then—real, unguarded, and messy.

Not the tears of someone caught in a lie.

But of someone who had loved badly... and lost badly.

Gertrude let out a soft, questioning quack, as if asking a question none of us could answer.

This was not what a cold, calculating murderer looked like.

I exhaled slowly.

But something about Rita's anger—the way it kept slipping into guilt—left a quiet unease in the back of my mind.

And I had learned long ago never to ignore that feeling.

I set a cup of coffee in front of Anne and sat down beside Junie in the teachers' lounge. Rita had left without demanding anything else, offering only a soft, shaken apology on her way out.

Anne looked now like someone who had been holding a door shut for too long and had finally let go. Devastated. Confused. Carrying questions that only Lionel could have answered—and a few I suspected no one ever would.

Gertrude hopped up onto the chair beside me, settled herself with a huff, and tucked her feet neatly beneath her. She watched Anne with steady, unblinking interest.

"Anne," I said, keeping my voice calm and even, "help me understand how this could have happened. Did you notice anything unusual with the enrollments? Anything at all?"

Anne wrapped both hands around her mug and leaned closer to the table. "I can't be sure, Tony, but..." She glanced around the room and lowered her voice, even though we were alone. "I don't believe Miss Lopez was having an affair with Mr. Hudson."

Junie frowned. "What about the note Rita mentioned? Do you think she made it up? She sounded sincere."

Anne shook her head. "No. I don't think Rita was lying." She hesitated. "I remember making a dinner reservation for Mr. Hudson a couple of weeks ago. At the time, I didn't think anything of it." Her eyes flicked to me. "I didn't—until today."

Gertrude quacked softly once, as if filing that away.

"I think it's something more than an affair." Anne gestured for us to lean closer. She waited until we did before continuing. "Miss Lopez was assigned to conduct an annual internal enrollment audit."

Junie gasped and clapped a hand over her mouth.

I didn't react—not outwardly. Something about it felt too neat. Too convenient.

"Is this the first year she's done it?" I asked lightly.

"Well—yes," Anne said quickly. Too quickly. "She was hired this year."

That didn't sit right.

You don't assign a sensitive audit to someone brand new—not unless you want fresh eyes. Or unless you already know what they're going to find.

"And who handled it before this year?" Junie asked.

Anne sighed and bit her lip. "That's the thing." She hesitated, then admitted, "This is the first year we've done an internal audit like that. Mr. Hudson requested it a few weeks ago—right after the Parents' Board appreciation meeting."

Gertrude shifted on the chair, feathers ruffling, clearly unimpressed by the timing.

"So Lionel asked for an audit before any of this came to light," I said slowly. "Before anyone was accused."

Anne nodded.

That changed things. Why would Lionel ask for an audit if he knew something was wrong with the records? So far, I had assumed he must have known about the fraud—but now I wasn't so sure.

"Do you know where we can find Miss Lopez?" I asked.

Because suddenly, speaking with her wasn't just curiosity.

It was necessary.

Chapter 8

Junie, Gertrude, and I were halfway up the walk to Miss Marina Lopez's house when the front door flew open and raised voices reached us.

"Get out! I have nothing to say to you!"

Penelope Whitcomb appeared on the porch, notebook in one hand, pen poised like a weapon. Even from the sidewalk, I could see that familiar smirk, and my stomach twisted.

I might have come here to ask difficult questions—but at least I wasn't planning to turn them into headlines for the entire town before anyone had proof.

"Is that your official statement?" Penny said smoothly. "And what about the student records that don't match the enrollment data? Did you miss those too?"

"I said get off my property!" Miss Lopez shouted. Whether it was anger or fear, her voice shook with it.

That was all I needed.

I leaned down and patted Gertrude's head. "You see the woman with the glasses?" I said softly. "We don't like her. Please escort her away."

Gertrude didn't hesitate.

She hopped onto the roof of my car, gave one powerful flap of her wings, and sailed straight onto the porch.

"And how exactly did you afford this house?" Penny was saying when Gertrude landed neatly between them.

Both women jumped back.

Gertrude turned slowly toward Penny, lifted her wings to their full, impressive span, and flapped forward with a series of sharp, authoritative quacks.

Penny screamed.

Not a dignified scream, either.

She turned and bolted down the path, nearly tripping over her own shoes as Gertrude followed her halfway to the sidewalk, wings out, head bobbing with purpose.

It was... magnificent.

I shouldn't have laughed. I truly shouldn't have.

But I did.

Junie laughed too, clutching her purse like she might drop it.

Penny reached her car, fumbled for the door, and finally noticed us standing there.

"Tony!" she shouted. "You and your bird are a menace to this city!"

Gertrude responded by taking two very deliberate steps in her direction.

Penny got into her car and drove off in a hurry.

I laughed harder.

It was ironic, really—that we were the menace to Apple Creek, not her reckless accusations and poorly sourced articles.

"Is that your duck?"

I turned to see Miss Lopez standing at the edge of the path, arms wrapped tightly around herself. Her face was pale, her eyes wary.

"This is Gertrude," I said. On cue, Gertrude puffed up proudly, every inch the professional bouncer. "Miss Lopez?"

She glanced from Gertrude to me.

"This is Miss Junie McCarthy," I added, gesturing behind me. "And I'm Miss Tony—"

"Miss Tony Cooper," she said quietly. "Mr.

Wilkins told me you might come by." She hesitated, then stepped aside. "Would you like to come in?"

Junie, Gertrude, and I followed her inside.

As soon as the door closed behind us, my heart began to pound. For the first time, the thought crossed my mind that I might be standing inside the home of someone capable of murder.

Miss Lopez looked frightened, exhausted —human.

But then again, most people do.

Arthur's words about Lionel's death flickered through my thoughts, and I made a quiet decision not to accept anything offered—not coffee, not water, not even a cookie.

Gertrude waddled ahead of us, inspecting the floor like she always did, entirely unbothered.

I wished I felt the same.

"Please, take a seat," Miss Lopez said, moving a pile of books off an old couch and pushing a basket of laundry aside from a chair before sitting down herself.

I smiled and did as she suggested, taking in the room as I settled. The furniture was old but well cared for—the kind of care that comes from love rather than money. The house was small, too. I doubted the second floor held more than two bedrooms.

Penny's parting remarks had no foundation at all.

"It was my grandmother's," Miss Lopez said, catching my glance. Her smile was sad, but affectionate. "She left it to my mother. My parents live in Maple Hollow, so they let me move in."

An explanation I hadn't asked for—but one that opened the door to trust.

"I don't believe anything Penelope Whitcomb was implying," I said gently. "But I do need to ask, Miss Lopez—when did Harold talk to you about me?"

"Please, call me Marina." She sighed, eyes dropping to her hands as she twisted her fingers together. "I ran into Harold yesterday. In the archive."

"Why were you in the archive?" I asked—then answered myself. "You knew about the fraud."

Her head snapped up. "That's why I quit.

I'm not a criminal. I wanted nothing to do with it."

"You're the whistleblower," Junie blurted.

Marina shook her head hard, her voice cracking. "No. I'm not."

She took a moment, breathing through it.

"About a month ago, I started hearing rumors about me going out with Mr. Hudson. I didn't like it and tried to talk to him about it. He agreed with me and said he would put an end to them. Then, about three weeks ago, he asked me to review the enrollment numbers—for this year and projections for next year. He said it was important because the numbers would determine whether the school qualified for the addition grant, and because I had been so direct with him about the gossip, he trusted me with it."

She grabbed a tissue from the box on the table. "The enrollment numbers were wrong. Way off. According to the files, I was supposed to have nearly double the students in my grade."

Gertrude shifted beside me, feathers ruffling.

"I thought it might be a duplication error," Marina continued. "But when I showed Mr. Hudson, he just nodded. He told me to take the next day and write a full report at home."

Her eyes filled again. "When I came back to school, everyone was talking about me—about how I'd taken a day off with Mr. Hudson, and how now I was his favorite." She swallowed. "I was scared. The rumors felt like a threat. So I quit."

I stood up too quickly, the thought pressing at me before I could sort it properly.

"He didn't stop you," I said slowly. "He didn't dismiss the report or try to smooth the numbers over. He asked you—someone new, someone clean—to look at it."

I folded my arms, uneasy now.

"And when you found something wrong," I added, "he sent you home to write it. Quietly."

The room felt suddenly smaller.

"If Lionel Hudson was trying to hide something," I said at last, choosing my words carefully, "this wouldn't have been the way to do it."

Gertrude gave a soft, questioning quack.

"I hate to say this," Junie said softly, "but Harold could've been involved then. He could have known, too. That's why Lionel was at his house."

Before I could answer, Marina shook her head.

"No," she said firmly. "Mr. Wilkins didn't do this."

We all looked at her.

"That's why I knew you'd come," she said. "Yesterday, when I saw Mr. Wilkins in the archive, I panicked—he was Mr. Hudson's friend—but one look at him told me he had no idea about the fraud... or me reviewing the numbers. We spent hours going through records. It got worse." She met my eyes. "The enrollment numbers have been inflated for at least five years. Not just here. All three elementary schools. The middle schools, too."

My stomach dropped.

"There's nothing in the high school files," she added quietly. "That's when Harold said he wouldn't be surprised if you showed up. Whoever did this never touched your schools. They were afraid you'd notice."

I left Marina's house with more questions than answers—and a heavier burden than I'd expected.

Lionel had tried to do the right thing. Harold was counting on me.

And I had no idea where to start.

"Maybe the police should talk to her," Junie said as she climbed into the back seat.

For the first time all day, that sounded like relief.

"You're right," I said, starting the car. "There's a detective I need to speak to. But you can't come with me."

"What? Why?" Junie groaned. "I can't go home, Tony—Bob is there."

I chuckled. "This may be the perfect opportunity to set boundaries. And the detective I need might arrest you if she sees you."

Junie sighed. "Maybe jail is better than home these days."

Gertrude quacked, sounding very much like she agreed.

Chapter 9

When I walked into the police station, I found Chief Ben Morales waiting near the front desk.

I wasn't there to ask about Harold, but when Ben asked me to follow him into his office and quietly offered to let me see my friend, I didn't argue—not even when he added that he was doing it to prevent me from "making trouble in the station."

That, apparently, was my reputation.

Ten minutes later, I was sitting in one of those small interview rooms with the large mirror on the wall.

Do they truly believe we don't know it's a window? Are we meant to assume criminals require constant reassurance about their appearance?

The door opened.

"Tony!" Harold exclaimed.

It had only been a day since I'd seen him, but he looked years older. He needed a shave. His clothes were wrinkled. Dark circles bruised the skin beneath his eyes, and his hands trembled as he moved.

"Harold," I said, stepping closer. "Have they tortured you? Are they starving you? Or are you ill?"

It was ridiculous—but he looked that bad.

He shook his head and attempted a smile. The officer who escorted him in helped him into the chair.

I noticed he wasn't handcuffed.

"You should tell Mr. Wilkins he needs to eat," the officer said gently. "And wear the jacket his wife brought him. Otherwise, you're right—he will get sick."

Then he left us alone.

"Nathan Hardison," Harold said quietly. "He's a young, good officer. Everyone here has been... considerate. Even for a criminal."

I crossed my arms. Now I understood why Ben had allowed the visit.

"What is your plan, Harold?" I asked. "Getting ill in here won't help anyone. You need your strength. We will prove your innocence."

"How did I miss it, Tony?" he interrupted, his hands shaking harder now. "Years. The fraud goes back years. And I never saw it." His voice cracked. "It's no wonder the high school records are the only ones in order. You wouldn't have missed it. You should be the superintendent. The district needs someone honest to clean this mess."

It was meant as a compliment, but I didn't accept it.

"Harold," I said firmly, "you know I would never take that position. I don't have the patience for school board politics or council meetings."

He tried to speak again, but I didn't let him.

"And it is not my job to clean this mess," I continued. "It's yours. And you will. But first, we need you out of here."

His shoulders sagged.

"What happened in your house?"

The tremor returned to his hands.

"I don't know," he whispered. "He was just there. And I thought—he's hurt, he's bleeding, do something." He swallowed hard. "So I took the knife out. I didn't think. I wasn't thinking." His breathing quickened. "What if that's what killed him? What if he would've—" He shook his head. "What if I'm the reason he..."

He couldn't finish the sentence.

I reached across the table and took his hands in mine.

"Start from the beginning," I said gently. "You called me from the archives. When did you leave?"

He swallowed and nodded.

"Around four-thirty. Marina had left maybe half an hour earlier. Did I tell you she was there? Have you spoken to her?"

"I talked to her, but you didn't mention her before," I said carefully. "But we'll get to that. What happened next?"

"I knew I was meeting you before the council session, so I went home to change. Beatriz wasn't there—she had one of her massage appointments. She moved it up because of the stress." He gave a tired smile. "Poor Bety. This has been hard on her."

I didn't say anything, but if Wallace had been accused of fraud, the last thing I would be thinking about was a massage appointment. Then again, I knew Beatriz. She felt everything deeply—sometimes too deeply—and stress had a way of undoing her.

Harold continued, "I walked into the kitchen to grab something to eat when I heard something fall upstairs. I called out for Beatriz —I thought perhaps she'd come home early, and I didn't want to startle her."

His breathing grew uneven.

"Then I heard something heavier. From the other side of the hallway. I rushed out of the kitchen, thinking she'd fallen." He stared at the table now, no longer seeing me. "When I passed the office, I saw a man in a suit lying face down."

His voice lowered.

"At first I didn't even recognize him. I was still looking for Beatriz." He swallowed. "I stepped inside. I saw the knife. And I thought —if I removed it, if I did something—"

He squeezed his eyes shut.

"I pulled it out, Tony. I thought I was helping."

I hesitated.

My fingers tightened slightly around Harold's hands, but I didn't tell him about the poison.

Not yet.

Harold was barely holding himself together as it was. Giving him hope—real hope, the kind that could pull him out of this room—

only to have it taken away if I was wrong... no. I wouldn't do that to him.

Not until I was certain.

"The blood touched my hands," he whispered, looking at his fingers. "But he didn't move. That's when I realized it was Lionel."

He covered his face.

"I didn't kill him... or maybe when I moved the—he was my friend."

I believed him. More now than ever.

"What about the front door?" I asked. "Did you notice it was open?"

He shook his head.

"No. I parked in the garage. I never looked at the front. I remember you mentioning it, and I kept thinking—how did I miss that?"

"And you didn't see anyone leaving? No car? No movement?"

He leaned forward slightly.

"I didn't have time to look. You were there, and then the police arrived." He hesitated. "But I've been thinking... what if the first thing I heard fall wasn't an accident? What if that was the killer leaving?"

Silence settled between us.

The idea pressed against my thoughts, unwelcome but unavoidable. Harold's description didn't match what I'd imagined.

Something about the timing unsettled me.

Harold pulling the knife out explained the blood.

It did not explain the knife.

I told Chief Ben what Harold had shared with me. He didn't look surprised.

He asked about Harold's state of mind, and I told him the truth. Harold was shaken, yes. Guilty over the fraud. Horrified about Lionel. But not murderous. Not calculating. Just a good man who had made a panicked mistake trying to help someone.

Pulling a knife out in desperation did not make you a killer.

I hadn't forgotten I'd come to speak with Detective Green about Marina's story, but since I was already inside the station, I asked Ben if I could stop by Arthur's office.

Working as a medical examiner did not lend itself to casual visitors.

As I made my way down the hallway, I found myself thinking how much nicer it would be to be outside in the sun with Gertrude, and how heavy it must feel to work in the basement of this old building day after day.

Then I heard laughter.

I recognized the voice immediately.

When I reached Arthur's doorway, Detective Green stood inside his office, pushing her hair back as she laughed at something my son had said.

My stomach tightened before I could stop it.

"I hope this isn't how you discuss your cases," I said.

It came out sharper than intended.

Arthur straightened at once. "Mom—what are you doing here? Ben will—"

"Ben let me in," I said, trying to sound calm. "And it's fortunate I found you both. Saves me time."

"Ben let you—what? Why?" Arthur asked.

Detective Green answered for me. "I asked him to let your mom visit Harold if she came by the station."

Once again, that wasn't what I had expected of her.

Arthur and I asked in unison, "Why?"

Arthur looked at me for a second, then added, "How did you know my mom would be coming?"

She gave my son a sideways smile that was entirely pleasant—and entirely inappropriate for how much I didn't want to like her. It softened her face and made her look younger—almost harmless.

Which irritated me more than it should have.

"I didn't know you would be coming," she said, turning her attention to me. "But after hearing Arthur speak about you—and how you helped your husband with his investigations—I thought you might want to see your friend Harold. I still hope you might decide to help with the fraud side of things."

Clever.

Too clever.

"So you were using my friend as bait?" I asked.

"Mom!" Arthur groaned.

Detective Green didn't bristle. "I used what I knew," she said plainly. "Harold is deteriorating by the hour. I'm concerned he might confess to something he didn't do just to end the pressure."

That caught my attention.

"Then why not release him?" I asked.

She exhaled slowly. "Because I think he may be safer here."

The room shifted.

"You think someone might hurt him?" I asked.

"I don't know," she admitted. "But this case is layered. And what Arthur discovered complicates things."

I looked to my son. "What did you discover?"

Arthur ran a hand through his hair and pressed his mouth shut.

"She already knows the knife wasn't the primary cause," Detective Green said.

"Tricia," Arthur warned.

"I can't involve my mom in a homicide investigation," he said firmly. "She may have helped my dad before, but it's different. She wasn't in any danger. This murder happened at her workplace. One of her friends is the prime suspect. No."

I softened slightly.

Detective Green turned back to me. "I'm sorry. Arthur's right. I don't want to put you at risk." She paused. "But I do need help understanding how enrollment manipulation could go unnoticed—how it works structurally. That's your expertise."

For someone as sharp as Detective Green, the mechanics of fraud couldn't possibly be that mysterious. It sounded like an excuse—but I was curious enough to indulge it. Plus, I wanted to talk about Marina Lopez's story with her anyway.

And, if I was being entirely honest with myself, I didn't mind the idea of Detective Green pressing against Arthur's professional boundaries. Maybe he would get mad at her.

"Well," I said slowly, "that is why I'm here."

She smiled. "Then perhaps we can—"

Her phone rang.

She stepped aside to answer it, and Arthur immediately leaned toward me.

"You need to be careful," he said quietly. "I don't like this case. And I don't want to call Dad because something happened to you while I'm taking care of you."

"You are so sweet, Arthur," I said lightly. "But I can still tie my own shoes."

"That's not what I meant."

I touched his cheek.

"I know."

Detective Green returned. "I need to check on something. Would you mind meeting me in half an hour? I haven't eaten all day. Would you like to grab something with me?"

I realized then that I hadn't eaten since my

early breakfast, and the suggestion sounded very good at the moment.

"That would be lovely," I said. "Gertrude and I can meet you at the bakery. Have you ever tried the bread bowl soup? It is glorious, Detective Green."

She tilted her head with a smile. "Please call me Tricia. And no—but I'm officially intrigued."

"Excellent." I walked toward the door. "I'll see you over there, Tricia."

As I walked toward the door, a quiet thought followed me.

Detectives do not invite outsiders into their cases without purpose.

I liked that she had asked for my help. I liked that she respected what I knew.

But I also noticed how easily she had smiled at Arthur.

It might have been strategy.

It might have been something else.

I wasn't sure yet which one it was.

But I would be paying attention.

Chapter 10

Prue Berry was the owner—and undisputed genius—behind Apple Creek's bakery. She was also a friend from our school days, which meant she always kept a small table for me near the patio doors at the back.

That way, Gertrude could linger outside without disturbing customers.

Gertrude loved the arrangement.

She was entirely too fond of dropped crumbs and inappropriate carbohydrates.

"Tony," Prue said as soon as I stepped inside, "you just missed it."

Unlike Junie, Prue was not given to dramatics. If she said I'd missed something, I had.

"What happened?"

She didn't answer right away. Instead, she

gestured for me to follow her and led me to my usual table near the patio. Gertrude waddled proudly behind us, already scanning the ground for opportunities.

Prue sat down across from me.

That alone told me this was serious.

The bakery wasn't as crowded as in the morning rush, but there were still enough customers that she should have been busy.

"Beatriz came in to pick up pastries," Prue began. "We were talking about Harold and the investigation when Anne Sullivan walked in."

She lowered her voice.

"I got lost in the school talk. Papers. Enrollment files. Who would take over the elementary school." She shook her head. "And I said—without thinking—that maybe Anne should step in as principal for the rest of the term."

That hadn't crossed my mind yet.

I'd been focused on fraud and murder. But Prue wasn't wrong. Someone would have to lead the school.

"That's not unreasonable," I said.

"That's what I thought," Prue replied. "But Beatriz did not."

Gertrude gave a low, curious quack.

"She snapped, Tony. Said it was Anne's negligence that allowed the fraud to happen in the first place. That Anne hadn't supervised the files properly."

I stiffened. "That's inappropriate. Is Anne all right?"

Prue nodded slowly. "She didn't take it quietly. She yelled back."

Anne. Yelled.

"She accused Beatriz," Prue continued carefully, "of benefiting from some study connected to the council. I didn't understand the details, but she said Beatriz's company was involved in what she called a 'City Council scandal.'"

My pulse ticked up.

"And then—" Prue hesitated for a second and lowered her voice, "she told Beatriz that if someone was going to clean up corruption in Apple Creek... she might want to watch her back."

Gertrude stopped pecking at the ground and lifted her head.

Anne had been in Apple Creek for years. Gentle. Methodical. Easily flustered by Penny Whitcomb, let alone a confrontation.

This was not like her.

"What did Beatriz do?" I asked quietly.

"She went pale," Prue said. "Grabbed her box and left. I think she was crying."

"And Anne?"

"She apologized to me for the scene." Prue folded her arms. "Then she told me she was scared."

"Of what?"

"Of being next."

The words hung between us.

"She thinks Lionel was killed because he knew about the fraud," Prue said softly, "and that whoever did it won't stop with him."

Gertrude shifted closer to my chair, brushing against my ankle.

"I told her that sounded dramatic," Prue added. "Why would she fear something like that if she didn't know anything?"

I nodded slowly.

It was the same question pressing at the back of my mind. Fear like that doesn't grow out of nothing.

The bell above the bakery door chimed, and Detective Green stepped inside.

"Sorry I'm late, Miss Tony," she said as she approached. "I had something to check on. I hope I haven't missed that famous bread bowl soup."

Prue stood immediately, her expression smoothing into professional brightness.

"Of course not," she said. "Tony insists it's life-changing. I'll bring two."

Gertrude eyed Tricia thoughtfully.

Which, I realized, was exactly what I was doing too.

I slid into the chair and patted Gertrude's head when she waddled up beside the table and settled herself near my feet.

"Is she all right?" Tricia asked, glancing toward the kitchen. "She seems... nervous."

"No, she is fine," I said lightly. "Do you come here often?"

I changed the subject on purpose. Prue had looked unsettled earlier, and I wasn't ready to share that just yet.

Tricia smiled. And if Arthur had feelings for her, I could see why.

"Detective Logan loves this place," she said. "When we worked together, we ended up here more than we should have. He's obsessed with Prue's pavlovas."

"That's reason enough," I said. "Where is he? I haven't seen him near City Hall."

"Florida," she replied, letting Gertrude inspect her fingers without flinching. "His father fractured his leg snorkeling with manatees."

I shook my head. "At some point, we must accept gravity."

She laughed. It was unforced.

"Logan is a troublemaker," I said, "but he's a good son. Is his absence why you were assigned this case?"

A flicker crossed her face—not insecurity, but something close.

"I don't think so," she said. "But I don't want it to be the reason I'm not trusted with complicated cases once he's back."

I nodded.

I liked that answer, even when I wasn't ready to admit it out loud.

"Well," I said, "let's see what we can untangle. What exactly do you need from me?"

Relief crossed her expression—brief but genuine.

"As I understand it," she began, "the elementary school addition grant was based on enrollment projections. Higher projected numbers justify expansion funding. Correct?"

"Correct," I said. "More students, more space needed, more grant eligibility."

She leaned forward. "So, is any money actually missing yet? I understand how inflated enrollment would increase funding. But this expansion project never even broke ground. So where, exactly, would the money have gone?"

Prue arrived with two bread bowls and placed them down with theatrical care—and clearly with an opinion about our conversation.

"Tony," she warned playfully, "behave. This is a paying customer."

I rolled my eyes.

"Without getting into my personal opinions about how this town loves to complicate simple things," I said, glancing toward the kitchen where Prue had already warned me to behave, "this is what happened."

I leaned forward.

"When a school might need more classrooms, the district doesn't just count desks and ask the teachers. Oh no. We commission a capacity study. Then a master facilities plan. Then community engagement sessions where everyone says the same thing three different ways."

Tricia's pen moved quickly.

"All of that gets paid for before a single brick is laid," I continued. "Taxpayer money. Real money. To determine whether we might need something we already know we need."

I lifted my hands.

"Could we have walked down the hallway and asked Anne Sullivan if the school was full? Yes. Would she have known? Absolutely. So would every teacher in that building."

I sat back with a small huff.

"But that would be too efficient. And efficiency rarely survives contact with City Hall."

Tricia's mouth twitched, but she didn't interrupt.

"That study," I went on more carefully now, "was conducted by Beatriz's firm. Their recommendation is what pushed the proposal to the council. The project stalled there—but the study? The master plan? Those were already completed."

"And paid for," Tricia said quietly.

"And paid for," I agreed. "At the sum of $1 million just for the study. I don't know about the master plan."

That's when it clicked.

Anne hadn't been shouting nonsense.

Beatriz's company had benefited before anyone laid a foundation. The developer had too.

The expansion never happened.

But the money had already moved.

"Have you spoken to Beatriz about that?" I asked.

"I asked about her whereabouts during the murder," she said. "The fraud is technically outside my scope unless I can connect it to the homicide."

"That's absurd," I said. "You think they're unrelated?"

"I think," she said calmly, "that I need proof before I make that leap. There was nothing in Harold's home tying him directly to the fraud."

"What about Lionel?" I pressed. "He is part of the fraud and was murdered in that house."

"That's the problem," she replied gently. "He was found in Harold's house, not in the school or the district's office."

The question lingered between us.

Gertrude shifted and tapped her beak lightly against Tricia's shoe.

"Why was Lionel in Harold's house?" I asked.

"That," she said, "is the question keeping me awake."

There was no smugness in her voice. Only frustration.

I lowered mine. "What about Beatriz and her company?"

Tricia didn't answer immediately.

Instead, she wiped her hands on her napkin and looked out toward the patio for a second. Not avoiding the question—measuring it.

"Her firm is clean on paper," she said at last. "The contracts are legitimate. The study exists. The invoices match the scope of work. If the fraud happened, it came from the district's side..." She bit her bottom lip and lowered her eyes. "Sorry."

"It's not your fault," I said. "If the district did it, that's on them. What about the murder?"

"She has an alibi," she said, but it was clear she didn't like it.

"The massage," I muttered.

Tricia nodded.

I leaned closer.

"But we know the knife wasn't what killed him."

Her expression shifted slightly.

"We don't know that definitively," she said quietly.

I blinked. "Arthur said something about the blood flow."

"He said the wound didn't behave as expected," she corrected. "He's still working on toxicology. The substance he found is difficult to identify."

"Substance?" I whispered. "Not poison?"

She pressed her lips together for a second. "From what I know today, Lionel could have ingested something contaminated—unintentional... or not. We don't know for sure yet."

Gertrude gave a small, dissatisfied quack.

"However, the knife," Tricia continued, "proves someone wanted him dead. Whether they succeeded with it or not is irrelevant. That person wanted him gone."

I gasped and sat back slowly. I hadn't thought about it like that.

This wasn't a tidy murder. It wasn't even a tidy fraud.

It was a mess.

Gertrude seemed to agree. She stopped inspecting Tricia's shoe and settled quietly at her feet.

Chapter 11

After talking with Tricia, I realized I'd been far too casual about the study.

For months, it had been the favorite topic of debate in the school district—ever since the expansion plan was announced. Small talk by the coffee machine. Heated debates in the copy room. Bullet-point updates in our weekly meetings.

Since it didn't technically belong to my part of the job, I treated it like an optional memo and quietly filed it under "not today."

Until now.

If I was going to understand what was really happening, I needed someone who lived for the deep side of the city.

No one was better than my dear friend

Martha Laurens—one of Apple Creek's council members and a fan of Gertrude.

Martha greeted us at her door with her usual warmth—and a story already halfway told—despite the late hour.

"Gertrude! Tony! You won't believe who I ran into at the pharmacy—"

Gertrude waddled straight past her without invitation, claws clicking against the hardwood as though she'd been summoned for official business.

Martha blinked. "Well. Good afternoon to you too, Gertrude."

Gertrude gave a single quack that sounded suspiciously like, *Proceed.*

Martha had always believed that a visit should be properly seasoned with context. High school had only sharpened that trait. Serving on the council had perfected it.

Most days, I adored her stories.

Today, I was on a mission.

"Martha," I said gently but firmly, interrupting her tale about living a full year just two streets away from her first ex-husband, Todd. "I need your help."

She paused mid-sentence without offense. One of the many reasons I loved her.

"What do you know about the school's fraud?" I asked bluntly.

Gertrude, who had discovered a decorative basket of pinecones, selected the largest one and began aggressively investigating it with her beak.

Martha's expression shifted. Thoughtful.

"We discussed it Monday," she said slowly. "Harold presented the numbers. I couldn't believe what I was seeing, Tony. But the figures don't lie. What we were shown looked... sketchy."

I disliked that word. *Sketchy* was small-town poison. Not strong enough to convict, but perfect for ruining anyone's reputation.

"Do you know who the whistleblower is?" I asked.

She shook her head. "All we saw were the documents sent to the Gazette."

Gertrude dropped the pinecone and wandered toward Martha's desk in the corner of the living room.

I stayed quiet. Silence is one of the best tools a woman can use.

It took three seconds for Martha to fill it.

"There's a list of students missing documentation—birth certificates, proof of residence, guardian contacts. Hundreds of them.

And some of the names are duplicated across multiple schools."

A small, surprising flicker of relief passed through me.

"So the reason it looks so widespread," I said carefully, "is because the same students appear more than once?"

"I believe so." She pressed her lips together. "I probably shouldn't tell you this."

That, of course, meant she would.

"Mayor Dosal asked Harold for a complete district-wide roster after the meeting. Every student. Every grade. He wants it cross-referenced to confirm who's real, who's enrolled, and where."

That was sensible. Logical.

Which made me wonder why Harold hadn't already requested it from Junie. She was in charge of registrations and enrollments, and it would be better for Harold if he didn't think Junie was involved in the fraud.

"I don't believe Harold orchestrated anything," Martha added, her tone softening. "I just don't know how he missed it."

Gertrude made her way back and settled beside Martha on the couch.

"Well, hello, pretty lady," Martha said, scratching the top of my sweet duck's head.

"If we follow the money..." I said—and yes, I borrowed the phrase shamelessly.

Martha gave me a look.

"The developer has already been paid," I continued. "And the company that conducted the study."

She sighed.

"The city pays the developer monthly," she said. "They handle all our master plans. In the long run, it's cheaper than hiring separately for each project. And all of our budget reports mention it."

"We pay them every month?" I asked, doing my best not to sound like a disgruntled taxpayer.

Martha gave a small nod. "It sounds worse than it is. You can't approve anything without a master plan. Schools, recreation programs, zoning adjustments. We'd spend more without a standing contract."

Lucky for my friend, I wasn't here to debate municipal budgeting.

"So the developer gained nothing extra from this particular expansion?"

"Nothing beyond the usual payment."

"And the study company?"

This time, Martha looked away.

Gertrude, sensing the shift, grew still.

"You think the fraud is tied to them?" I asked quietly. "This is Beatriz's company."

"I know." Her voice was steady, but something underneath it trembled. "I didn't support hiring her from the start. Lionel and Beatriz were close. That should have raised a conflict-of-interest concern."

That stopped me.

"Beatriz was close to Lionel?"

"It was his recommendation. They worked long hours on the study. My office at the Community Center is right down the hall from the research room. I saw them."

I was still processing what she was implying when Tricia's comment came to mind.

"The police reviewed the study. They found nothing wrong," I said.

"I know," Martha replied. "Which is why I didn't press further."

Gertrude gave a low, questioning quack.

Martha absently stroked her back.

"Tony, between us, I don't believe the study is clean. Something doesn't sit right with me about this one."

I didn't say it out loud, but I agreed with Martha.

It didn't sit right with me either.

That night, making dinner proved to be a challenge.

My mind was everywhere except the kitchen, and the fish paid the price for it. The rice followed bravely behind.

By the time Arthur came home, I was standing on a chair, waving a dish towel at a cloud of smoke that had no intention of leaving.

Gertrude stood in the middle of the kitchen floor, issuing sharp, offended quacks as if she had personally warned me against over-cooking seafood.

"Yes, yes," I muttered. "I hear you."

Arthur opened the door, stopped short, and immediately grabbed another towel to help fan the air.

"What's going on?" he asked, coughing once as he waved the smoke toward the back door.

"Well," I said, stepping down from the chair with what dignity I could manage, "we don't have dinner."

I paused, then corrected myself. "Unless you enjoy fish that requires a legal disclaimer."

He laughed—bless him—and moved toward the stove without complaint. Even while scraping the pan, he studied me with quiet concern.

"Is this about your conversation with Tricia?" he asked. "Or this Harold person?"

I sat at the kitchen table, suddenly very tired.

"This Harold person," I said gently, "is a dear friend of mine, Arthur. And I'm worried about him. He doesn't look well. Not physically. And certainly not mentally. Stress does terrible things to people."

Arthur set a glass of water in front of me and leaned against the counter.

"Exactly, Mom. Stress does terrible things. And now I'm worried about you."

How could I not smile at that?

"I'm fine," I said. "Just distracted. There's too much swirling around. I can't let Harold sit in that cell—or worse, be charged with a murder I know he didn't commit. And then there's the fraud, and Junie is in danger there. It makes everything feel... sketchy."

Martha's words replayed in my head. Duplicate names. Study case. Conflict of interest.

One of the things I've always loved about my job is that, done properly, it ends at five o'clock. Of course, I've made mistakes over the years—we all have—but never the kind that follow you home and sit at your dinner table.

Gertrude waddled over and pecked lightly at Arthur's shoe, as if reminding him that some of us were still waiting for edible food.

"What did Tricia ask you?" Arthur said casually, pulling eggs and cheese from the refrigerator.

I blinked. "What are you doing?"

He glanced at his hands. "Cooking."

"I can cook," I protested weakly, starting to rise.

He shook his head and gently nudged me back into the chair.

"I've lived alone for a while, Mom. How do you think I survived? Frozen pizza and good intentions?"

I opened my mouth to answer and then closed it. That possibility had, in fact, crossed my mind.

"And don't avoid my question," he added. "What did you and Tricia talk about?"

It struck me then that Tricia hadn't told him. That surprised me more than it should have.

"She wanted to know how the school could have committed the fraud."

Arthur frowned. "Not the murder?"

I sighed. "She doesn't have proof they're connected, which is ridiculous. Of course they're connected. Coincidences aren't real."

He chuckled softly while working the eggs into a pan.

"Sometimes coincidences are real, Mom. That's what makes this job complicated."

I crossed my arms. "Did you figure out what killed Lionel?"

Arthur's shoulders tightened just slightly.

"No," he said. "And it isn't your job to figure that out. Let Tricia—"

"Arthur Cooper."

He froze mid-stir.

His full name still worked.

"Harold is my friend," I continued. "What would you do if Logan were sitting in a cell?"

He scrubbed a hand down his face and groaned.

"You are more stubborn than Maggie," he muttered. "I'm not even going to try to stop you."

Relief washed through me.

"So you'll help me?"

He set the spatula down and faced me fully.

"What do you know so far?"

Joy flickered inside me—sharp and bright. I had worked beside Wallace for years, but I was always the sounding board, the one who helped untangle his thoughts. This felt different.

"I know Harold didn't kill Lionel. And the fraud is a setup. The paperwork goes back years. But I don't understand how the study could be clean if—"

Arthur lifted both hands.

"Stop. You can't solve it by leaping to the end. Start at the beginning. What do you actually know?"

I hesitated.

He was right.

"Harold was found holding the knife," I said slowly. "But you mentioned the knife might not—"

"Mom." He pulled out a chair and sat across from me. "Listen carefully before you get upset. You believe Harold is innocent. That's not the same thing as knowing it. And I suspected something about the cause of death—but suspicion isn't proof. I have to wait for lab results."

That was fair.

Uncomfortable, but fair.

He reached across the table and took my hands.

"You know the district. You know the paperwork. You know how things are supposed to work. Focus on the fraud. Let Tricia handle the murder. If they're connected, your paths will cross at the right time."

Gertrude hopped up onto the table beside me—a maneuver she absolutely knew she wasn't allowed to perform—and settled there as if presiding over the meeting.

I sighed.

He was right.

I didn't like it, but he was right.

"But what if Tricia misses something?"

Arthur smirked. "Give her a chance."

He slid a plate of surprisingly beautiful scrambled eggs in front of me.

"Now," he said, leaning forward slightly, "tell me what you know about the fraud."

Gertrude quacked once.

Firmly.

As if demanding a proper report.

Chapter 12

Talking with Arthur the night before had been a clarity break.

I had been mixing the crimes together in my mind—murder and fraud—as if stirring them long enough would make sense of both. Instead, it had only clouded everything.

Arthur had asked one simple question:

Who benefits from the exposure of the fraud?

And the truth was, I didn't know.

I parked outside the Gazette and took a slow breath.

"All right, Gertrude," I said, feeling the heat rising in my chest. "We're going to be civil. We're going to be calm. And we are absolutely not going to peck anyone."

Gertrude blinked at me.

That was not a promise.

Arthur's question echoed again as we stepped inside.

If Lionel had planned to expose the fraud himself—as Marina suggested—then why was the information leaked first instead of through an official report like the one he had supposedly requested? And why to Penny?

A report would have brought the police and an investigation. The Gazette brought scandal—and maybe a murder.

"Good morning," I said sweetly to the receptionist, who immediately froze at the sight of my feathered companion. "I have some information about the district fraud and would like to speak with Miss Whitcomb."

The receptionist stared at Gertrude.

Gertrude stared back.

It was a silent contest of territory.

"And your name?" the receptionist asked cautiously.

"Miss Tony Cooper."

It took nearly fifteen minutes before Penny appeared.

She descended the hallway with a smile polished enough to reflect sunlight.

"Miss Tony," she said smoothly. "I can't say I'm surprised to see you. Though I expected more threats from you and your goose, not information."

Gertrude let out an indignant quack.

"She's a duck," I corrected calmly. "And what can I say? Life is full of surprises."

"I see that," Penny replied.

She led us into a large conference room and took the center seat at the long table.

Of course, I sat directly across from her.

Gertrude hopped onto the chair beside me without invitation and began inspecting the glossy tabletop as though searching for hidden breadcrumbs of corruption.

"What do you have for me, Miss Tony?" Penny asked.

I smiled pleasantly.

"The district is a mess at the moment. As you can imagine, losing a superintendent is challenging at any time of the school year—but this timing makes it especially difficult."

Penny shook her head slowly, folding her fingers together on the table.

"Let's not exaggerate. This isn't exactly a critical point in the academic calendar. Most of you are counting down to summer—playing computer games or gossiping your way to the last bell."

That worried me.

She might have been exaggerating about the gossip, but the comment about computer games felt uncomfortably specific. From time to time—strictly after my work was finished—I did indulge in a few harmless seek-and-find puzzles while waiting on paperwork from others.

Nothing criminal.

But Penny didn't say that randomly.

For her to mention it so precisely meant one thing.

She had someone inside the district.

And she wanted me to know it.

"And you would know that because of your whistleblower?" I asked lightly.

The satisfaction in her expression was impossible to miss.

"Wouldn't you like to know?"

Actually, yes.

But not in the way she thought.

"Not particularly," I said pleasantly. "But I imagine you'd be interested to know your information may not be accurate."

It was a bluff. A deliberate one.

After checking with Junie, I knew the discrepancies were real.

But Tricia had asked for my help because I understood how the district worked—a complicated process. Enrollment forms were filled, copied, transferred, archived, or transferred again. It had been known that mislabeled—and occasionally misplaced—files by well-meaning people who hadn't had enough coffee had happened.

If I questioned the validity of those files, my experience and reputation would carry more weight than evidence.

Gertrude chose that moment to peck decisively at the edge of the conference table. My reinforcement.

Penny's smile faltered.

"Not accurate?" she repeated a little too quickly.

"There is no fraud," I continued evenly. "What you saw were duplicated filing copies. Enrollment forms are archived in more than one location. A stack of extra folders in Harold's office doesn't mean anything."

Penny's posture shifted.

"I didn't just see folders," she said coolly. "I verified the documents. Missing birth certificates. Missing proof of residence. Duplicate student IDs. The enrollment totals don't match."

I chuckled. "You verified? The archive is a mess of—"

"In Harold's office, Tony!"

"You were inside Harold's office," I said quietly.

"I was given access."

Gertrude leaned forward and pecked at the glossy surface again—this time directly at Penny's reflection.

"But the numbers match the enrollment study," I said. "In your article, you only accused the district. Are you suggesting the study is fraudulent as well? Or did you forget to mention that in your gossip column?"

"The study is correct!" Penny raised her voice. "You don't get it," she said, leaning forward. "This will cost her everything—her job, her credibility, her place in this town. She wouldn't throw that away unless she was absolutely certain. She would never—"

Her.

There it was.

Gertrude gave a soft, thoughtful quack.

I kept my face neutral.

"You're trying to trick me into revealing my source," Penny said, regaining herself. "It won't work. She has protection from the justice system as a whistleblower. I admire her courage."

I made a mental note to verify that later but didn't waste time debating Penny.

"There is no protection from false accusations," I said quietly.

Penny slammed her palm against the table.

Gertrude exploded into outraged flapping, wings lifting as if prepared to defend the honor of Apple Creek.

"She isn't lying!" Penny snapped. "The fraud is real, and your friend is guilty of it."

"Harold?" I asked.

"Yes."

Then she leaned forward.

"Why don't you ask Beatriz about the study? Or are you afraid your other friend might be a criminal too?"

That hit harder than I expected.

Gertrude went still beside me.

If the whistleblower was a woman...

If she stood to lose her career...

If she had access to both district files and the study data...

Then Beatriz still fit.

But Penny had just pushed me toward her.

If Beatriz were the mastermind, Penny would never send me directly to her.

Unless she wanted me to—and she was being calculated.

Bluffing.

I stood slowly.

"Thank you for your time, Penny."

She smirked. "Careful, Tony. Truth has a way of biting."

Gertrude flapped once and knocked a pen off the table, hitting Penny's leg.

I didn't apologize.

As Gertrude and I stepped out of the Gazette, the pieces began rearranging themselves in my mind.

The whistleblower was a woman.

She had access to Harold's office.

She knew the district well enough to understand the filing system—and apparently well enough to know about my harmless computer games.

She believed the fraud was real.

Or wanted everyone else to believe it was.

She had something significant to lose.

And she either trusted whistleblower protection completely...

Or she didn't care about the consequences.

It was time to talk to Beatriz.

I reached for my phone.

It rang before I could dial.

"Tony," Junie whispered the moment I answered. "Are you coming into the office today? Please tell me you're already on your way."

"What is it, Junie? I thought you were home. Is this about Bob? You need to figure out how to live with—"

There was movement on the line.

And then I heard it.

Crying.

Not loud. Not dramatic. But painful.

A second later, Junie spoke again.

"Marina is here to see you. Please hurry. I don't know what to do."

Marina.

My heart tightened.

The last time I had seen her, she was shaken —but steady. I hadn't expected to hear from her again. Not like this.

Within the hour, I was walking into the district building.

Gertrude followed closely, her usual confident waddle subdued by the tension in my steps.

Junie met me at the entrance, holding an empty mug and wearing an expression I had only seen once before—the day Harold was arrested.

“She’s in your office,” Junie whispered. “I didn’t know where else to put her.”

I didn’t argue.

When Junie opened the door, I barely recognized Marina.

Her face was pale. Her eyes swollen. Her hair pulled back carelessly, as if she hadn’t looked in a mirror all morning. She looked smaller somehow.

Fragile.

“Miss Tony,” she said, her voice rough and uneven. “I needed to see you. I think I know—” She stopped, staring at Junie by the door.

“I’ll get you more tea, sweetie.” Junie slipped back out, closing the door softly behind her.

Gertrude moved closer to my desk, unusually quiet.

“What is it, Marina?” I asked gently.

Marina swallowed hard.

“I shouldn’t have let him do it,” she whispered. “I wasn’t entirely honest with you.”

My stomach tightened.

“It’s all right,” I said, in the calm tone I reserved for children in trouble. “You don’t know me, and things are scary right now. I understand. Just tell me what's bothering you. Who did what?"

She began coughing.

At first, it sounded like nerves—dry and shallow.

Then harsher.

I stepped closer, placing a hand on her shoulder.

"It's all wrong," she choked. "I told him it was too risky. Too dangerous—and it would ruin everything I discovered. He said it was the only way to fix it. To protect me."

"Fix what?" I pressed softly.

Another violent cough overtook her. She bent forward, gripping the edge of my desk.

Then I saw it.

A thin line of red at the corner of her mouth.

"Junie!" I called sharply. "Call an ambulance!"

Marina's hand shot out and grabbed mine with surprising force.

"I didn't know who she was until—" she gasped, her eyes fixed on something behind me. "I never thought she could— I trusted her—" more coughing— "she hid the report—she killed him—"

The rest dissolved into coughing.

Her body trembled once, then sagged.

"Marina?" I whispered.

Behind me, something shattered.

I turned—and felt a chill run through me when I realized who Marina had been looking at.

Junie stood frozen in the doorway, a broken mug at her feet.

"Tony, I didn't—I don't know why she said that. You know me."

I didn't have the chance to answer.

Tricia moved past her quickly, already kneeling beside Marina to check her pulse. The paramedics followed seconds later, purposeful and efficient. In less than a minute, my office no longer felt like mine.

It looked like Harold's house.

Minus the blood.

I stepped back as equipment bags opened and voices overlapped in low, urgent tones.

Gertrude pressed against my leg, letting out a soft, unsettled sound.

This had taken a turn I didn't like.

Not at all.

Chapter 13

I was sitting by the front desk of the department, holding Junie, who hadn't stopped crying since the incident, when Arthur rushed in.

He scanned the room quickly—officers, paperwork, tension—until his eyes landed on me.

"Mom." He crossed the room in three long strides. "Are you all right? What happened?"

I managed a small smile and took his hands.

"I'm fine," I said softly. "I just witnessed Marina die in my office."

Arthur's head snapped toward the hallway, then back to me.

"Marina? Who is she? Did she work here?"

I shook my head. "No. She used to teach at the elementary school."

"The one where the principal was murdered?"

Before I could answer, Tricia stepped out of my office, pulling off a pair of latex gloves as she approached us.

"There isn't much to go on," she said, her voice controlled but tight. "It could be illness. Your mom mentioned heavy coughing." She paused. "But given the circumstances... I doubt it."

Her eyes shifted between Arthur, Junie, and me.

"Did you know her well?"

Junie shook her head quickly, still trembling beside me.

"Not well," I answered carefully. "We visited her yesterday. Anne Sullivan mentioned Marina had resigned, and we wanted clarification about the fraud."

Arthur crossed his arms but stayed quiet.

Tricia's gaze sharpened.

"She was fired because of the fraud?"

I chose my words with care.

"She resigned after rumors spread about an affair with Lionel. She told us it wasn't an affair. Lionel had asked her to audit the school records. She discovered discrepancies and brought them to him, believing they were mistakes. He asked her to prepare a report about them. She was worried the rumors had gotten worse and felt threatened, so she quit."

Tricia absorbed that.

Then she looked directly at me.

"Did you know this when we spoke at the bakery?"

I hesitated.

She didn't wait for the answer.

"Where is the report?"

"I don't know," I said, bristling at her tone. "I wasn't about to search her home."

"Of course not," Tricia replied evenly. "But now she is dead, and maybe knowing about this report earlier could have saved her."

Arthur stepped slightly in front of me.

"You can't blame my mom for her death. She isn't a suspect."

Tricia's eyes hardened.

"I can question anyone who withholds relevant information in an active investigation."

Arthur stepped forward, pointing a finger.

"She wasn't withholding anything. She was trying to understand the fraud. Isn't that what you asked her to do?"

"I asked her to help me make sense of the

fraud, but this happened before I spoke to her. She should have told me about Marina so I could have formally interviewed her," Tricia countered. "Now she is dead."

Arthur's jaw tightened.

"Maybe your inexperience is what's making you doubt this case," he said, his voice tight. "No other detective would ask a witness for guidance. And no one would treat a concerned citizen like a liability."

At my side, Junie stopped crying.

Across the room, officers froze mid-step, mid-sentence, mid-breath.

Tricia straightened. When she spoke, her tone was calm—dangerously calm.

"I don't arrest people without evidence," she said evenly. "Apple Creek is a small town. A false accusation doesn't just damage a record—it damages lives."

Her eyes shifted briefly to me, then back to Arthur.

"We now have two deaths connected to the same district. I need confirmed causes of death before I build theories. That's procedure."

The air felt heavy.

"It's time you focus on your job, Arthur," she continued quietly. "Or should I request another medical examiner? Unlike me, you may be too close to this case to stay objective."

Arthur didn't respond.

He simply turned and walked toward my office, his shoulders stiff.

Tricia held my gaze a moment longer.

"You should have told me about the report," she said quietly.

Then she left the department.

The air felt thinner after she was gone.

I sat there, torn cleanly down the middle.

Arthur was my son.

No one speaks to him like that.

But Tricia was right about one thing.

I should have told her.

And now there were two bodies connected to the same story.

For the first time in my life, I had the chance to see what my son actually did at work.

Not that I hadn't imagined it before. I had. In my mind, the detective was always in charge of the scene—giving instructions, piecing things together—while the medical examiner worked quietly in the background.

I was wrong.

Arthur was the one directing the room.

"Finish the photographs and bag the fragments," he said, stepping carefully over the broken pieces of Junie's mug near the entrance. "I want the residue of the liquid tested."

His voice was steady. Controlled.

Maybe he was always like this. Or maybe the confrontation with Tricia had sharpened him.

I couldn't tell.

I moved closer to the doorway of my office, unable to stay seated any longer.

Arthur knelt beside Marina, examining her with clinical precision. Without turning around, he said,

"You shouldn't be here, Mom."

Several officers glanced at me.

I suddenly felt like a child caught peeking into a cupboard.

"This is my office," I said weakly. "I don't want people moving my things. You know how particular I am."

He looked up at me then.

The disapproval was there.

But so was something else.

Regret. Or pain. I couldn't tell.

"Fine," I said softly. "But tell me something. Do you think she was sick? That cough sounded terrible. She didn't look ill yesterday —nervous, yes. But not sick."

Arthur stood and pulled off his gloves.

"I need to run a full panel," he said. "Toxicology, pathology—everything. Until I have results, I can't say anything for certain."

I glanced toward the broken mug on the floor.

"Junie gave her tea," I said quietly. "Marina said 'she killed him' before she collapsed. She was looking toward the door. Junie was standing there."

Arthur stepped closer. His voice lowered.

"We both know Junie didn't poison her," he said gently.

"I know," I answered. "But what if the tea—"

"It's possible," he admitted. "Which is why it'll be tested."

The word possible lodged in my chest.

He rested his hands briefly on my shoulders.

"I'm not the detective," he said carefully. "And neither are you. Whatever you know— about the fraud, about Marina—Tricia needs it."

Then I understood. It was guilt for what he had said to her.

"It'll be all right." He tried to smile, but it only made him look sadder. "For now, you need to leave the scene. Your office or not."

I nodded and stepped away.

Junie followed me into the hallway, still trembling.

"How many cups of tea did you give her?" I asked gently.

"Just one," she whispered. "She wouldn't stop crying. She looked bad—maybe sick? I thought it was stress or fear. I didn't know what to do. I should have called an ambulance sooner, shouldn't I?"

"Oh, Junie," I said, squeezing her hand. "You were trying to help."

I could have stopped there. I could have gone home and let the professionals handle it.

Then I saw her.

Penelope Whitcomb burst through the lobby doors, notebook already open, calling questions at the nearest officer.

"How many fatalities now? Is this connected to the superintendent? Is the district covering something up?"

The officers looked overwhelmed.

And I knew, with absolute certainty, that if

I didn't get ahead of this, Penny would turn confusion into chaos before sunset.

I straightened my shoulders while Gertrude pressed close against my ankle.

We couldn't let that happen.

Chapter 14

I edged back toward the elevator wall, hoping to avoid Penny altogether.

Two officers moved quickly, blocking her path in the lobby. From a distance, I recognized Tricia's voice—calm, firm.

"This is a crime scene. You can't be here."

I gently steered Junie down the hallway toward the police department, but we weren't fast enough.

"She's here!" Penny shouted, pointing directly at me.

Tricia turned for a second, and something in her expression made my chest tighten.

It wasn't anger.

It was disappointment.

The same kind I had just seen in Arthur's eyes.

I didn't know what lived between them—whether it was simply respect strained by duty or something softer that neither of them had named yet.

But whatever this case was doing to them, it went deeper than procedure.

And I couldn't ignore the quiet suspicion that I had helped drive the wedge.

"I don't owe you an explanation," Tricia said, guiding Penny toward the exit. "You need to leave. Now."

Penny shifted tactics instantly.

"Do you have any comment on the investigation, Detective?" she called out loudly. "Or are we waiting for a third victim before you share anything with the public?"

It took all my willpower not to jump to Tricia's defense. I might not have liked her at the beginning, but Penny was out of line.

"How does she know?" Junie whispered as I ushered her farther inside the police department. "Who called the Gazette, Tony? Do you think she's involved?"

I shook my head.

"No. Penny lives for police scanners and loose-lipped officers. She doesn't need to be involved—she just needs noise."

Junie nodded, but when we stepped fully into the station lobby, her face drained of color.

"What are we doing in here?"

I turned to her and took both her hands.

"I need you to stay here. Listen. If you hear anything about Marina, Harold, or the fraud—anything at all—I need to know."

Her eyes widened.

"You're leaving?"

"I need to talk to Beatriz."

Junie's grip tightened instantly.

"Tony! If she's behind this, she's already killed two people!"

Her voice dropped to a whisper.

"What if she tries to—"

"I won't eat or drink anything," I said gently. "Pinky promise."

She did not look reassured.

"What about me?" she whispered. "What if Detective Tricia comes and arrests me?"

I inhaled slowly, keeping my voice steady.

"Whoever is responsible is still out there, Junie. And you know the district's filing system better than anyone. If Tricia were to arrest you —which she won't—you'd be safer in custody than alone."

Her eyes widened further.

"Tony, I do not want to be safer in custody."

I squeezed her hands.

"We're not getting to that," I said, perhaps with more confidence than I felt. "And look on the bright side—Bob can't argue with you from a holding cell."

That earned the faintest, reluctant sniff of a laugh.

Good.

I released her hands before she could protest again.

Tricia was still managing Penny near the entrance. I avoided the scene entirely and slipped out the side doors.

Gertrude waddled beside me with surprising determination.

"Come on," I murmured. "No more distractions."

The pieces were shifting.

Penny slipped that the whistleblower was a woman.

Marina also accused a woman.

And Martha didn't trust Beatriz's study.

"We're going to talk to Beatriz," I said. "It's overdue to hear her side of the story."

Gertrude gave one firm quack.

"Tony!" Beatriz exclaimed as she opened the door and immediately pulled me into a hug. "I wasn't expecting you, but I'm so glad you're here. Please, come in."

Gertrude hesitated on the threshold, craning her neck inside as if assessing the emotional climate. I gave her a look before stepping in.

I shouldn't have been surprised to find Beatriz in visible distress. Her husband was in jail. The fraud scandal was spreading through town like a summer wildfire. For a fleeting moment, I felt almost ashamed for coming with more questions.

"Forgive the mess," she said as we moved into the living room. "I haven't had the courage to go into the kitchen or—" her voice faltered just slightly—"the office."

That explained the takeout containers stacked neatly on the coffee table and the organized chaos of paperwork covering the couch cushions.

"Is it still sealed?" I asked carefully, glancing toward the hallway.

She shook her head. "The police released it

that night." A controlled inhale. "Do you know I'm responsible for cleaning it? I had to hire a biohazard company to remove..." She paused. Blinked. "Everything."

Her eyes filled, but the tears didn't spill immediately.

Gertrude waddled past us and began inspecting a stack of folders on the floor, nudging one with her beak before settling beside it.

"I can't even walk down that hallway," Beatriz whispered, lowering herself onto the couch and ignoring the papers crinkling beneath her. "Every time I close my eyes, I see it."

I sat opposite her, trying to steer clear of the chaos.

"Did you know Lionel well?"

She reached for a tissue.

"He worked closely with Harold. And with me, on the study." A pause. "We had a few meetings about the study and the expansion."

She looked toward the window.

"I can't understand why anyone would stab him like that." Her voice trembled, but her posture remained perfectly upright. "The idea that someone could stand behind you, waiting..." She pressed her hand to her chest. "It's unbearable."

Gertrude let out a soft, questioning quack.

Beatriz turned back to me abruptly.

"Marina Lopez was here this morning," she said.

My spine stiffened.

"She came in furious. Accusing me—accusing my company—of fraud."

She stood and moved toward the coffee table, shuffling papers deliberately.

"I told her I simply process the data the district provides. How could I fabricate information?"

She picked up a thick folder and handed it to me.

"She threw this at me."

Gertrude immediately stepped closer, pecking once at the corner before I took it.

Inside: student names. Highlights. Marginal notes. The word *duplicate* scrawled repeatedly in hurried handwriting.

"Beatriz, this needs to go to the police."

"I know," she said quickly—too quickly. Then softened. "But I thought... perhaps you could look at it first."

I shook my head, but she didn't let me speak.

"I trust you, Tony. You understand the district better than anyone. If this is nonsense from a distressed former teacher, you'll see it immediately."

Tricia had already asked me to look into the fraud. Hopefully, this would clarify things.

"Tony..." Beatriz lowered her tone. "There were rumors about her and Lionel," she added quietly. "An affair. Perhaps this is retaliation. Perhaps she and Lionel were involved in it together and—"

She stopped herself.

"I shouldn't speculate. I really don't know Marina. And although I didn't like her coming here and treating me like that, I understand. Harold is in prison, and I'm falling apart."

Slowly, I closed the folder.

"Beatriz," I said gently. "Marina is dead."

She stepped backward, shaking her head, her expression tightening.

"When?" she whispered. "How?"

"In my office. We don't know how yet."

Her hand flew to her mouth.

"Oh no," she breathed. "Now it will look like I silenced her." A pause. Then firmer: "Tony, I didn't."

I watched her carefully. There was panic in her eyes—as well as fear.

"I need that report given to the police, but I don't trust they will understand what it means the way you will," she said, regaining composure. "It may clear Harold. And it proves I have nothing to hide."

As she spoke, Gertrude slipped past me and waddled down the hallway.

I stood.

"I'll take this to the police," I said, lifting the folder. "I'll look at it first, then hand it over."

Beatriz bit her lip, then nodded.

I was about to leave when she stopped me.

"Tony, since Marina is dead, this may be important." She looked down. "I'm not sure if you knew this, but Rita had a relationship with Lionel—and was not happy about the rumors with Marina. I learned about it because Rita attended several of the study meetings. The Parents' Board had strong opinions about the expansion, but... well, Rita had a few sharp exchanges with Lionel."

She let the implication hang.

It was very clear.

And, unfortunately, it made sense.

Second Death Shakes Apple Creek as Investigation Expands

By Penelope "Penny" Whitcomb
Apple Creek Gazette

APPLE CREEK — The ongoing investigation into financial irregularities within the Apple Creek School District took a disturbing turn Friday after a second sudden death was reported—this time inside the district's administrative offices.

Marina Lopez, a former teacher at Creek Elementary School, collapsed earlier today while visiting the district office. Emergency services were called, but Lopez was pronounced dead at the scene.

Authorities have not confirmed a cause of death.

Detective Patricia Green, who is leading the investigation into both the financial discrepancies and the recent death of Principal Lionel Hudson, stated that "all possibilities remain under consideration" but declined to provide further details.

The circumstances surrounding Lopez's death have raised immediate concerns due to her recent connection to the district's ongoing inquiry.

Sources indicate that Lopez had been involved in reviewing student enrollment records shortly before her resignation from Creek Elementary. While officials have not confirmed the extent of her involvement, questions remain about what she may have uncovered—and whether that information is connected to the broader investigation.

Lopez's presence at the district office at the time of her death has also drawn attention.

While authorities have not released an official statement regarding the purpose of her visit, multiple individuals familiar with the situation suggest she may have been attempting to share information related to the enrollment discrepancies.

Unconfirmed reports indicate that several district employees were present at the time of the incident.

Though no wrongdoing has been established, the fact that two deaths are now linked —directly or indirectly—to the same district has left many residents unsettled.

"This isn't just a coincidence anymore," said one community member. "Something is happening, and no one is telling us what it is."

Concerns appear to be growing across Apple Creek, with some parents questioning whether those connected to the investigation may be at risk.

Officials have urged the public to remain calm and avoid speculation.

However, with few answers and a second unexplained death, speculation may be difficult to contain.

As of now, no official connection has been confirmed between Lopez's death, the financial investigation, and the earlier death of Principal Hudson.

The Gazette will continue to follow this developing story.

Chapter 15

Unlike what most people would assume, I didn't actually know where everyone lived in Apple Creek. Rita Carver was certainly not someone I spent my afternoons visiting. Before this week, the last thing I wanted was to socialize with the Parents' Board—especially its president.

So I drove back to City Hall first. I needed Rita's address.

And I needed to hand Tricia the report Beatriz had given me.

After her comments about withheld information—and after seeing what that tension had done to whatever stood between her and Arthur—the last thing I wanted was to wedge myself further between them.

But when I walked into the station, Tricia was gone and Arthur was mid-autopsy.

Which was something I did not need to see.

So I did the next reasonable thing.

I took Junie home with me. Our offices were crime scenes again.

My dining table would have to do.

Gertrude claimed the head of the table immediately, stepping onto Marina's report as though presiding over a council session.

"Madam Chair," I murmured, sliding the pages gently out from under her webbed feet.

"And Beatriz just handed this to you?" Junie asked as we spread the photocopies across the table. "I can't believe Marina would threaten her. Or anyone."

"You didn't know Marina before yesterday," I reminded her gently.

Junie's mouth trembled.

"She seemed kind. Now she's dead. And next, I'll be the suspect."

Small towns do not require proof to support whispers.

"Junie," I said softly, "we are not blaming

Marina. Wallace always told me—put emotion aside. Follow the facts."

Gertrude pecked twice at one of the papers.

"Exactly," I said, nodding at my faithful, feathery companion. "Let's find the facts."

After nearly an hour, one thing became clear: this wasn't a report in the traditional sense. It was a collection of photocopies—enrollment forms, student ID printouts, folio numbers, medical forms, allergy alerts, disciplinary notes—shuffled together with no visible order.

Messy.

If this was a sample of Marina's work, it spoke poorly of her professionalism.

"I understand duplicating paper files," Junie said, pushing her glasses up her nose. "Just add extra folders into the cabinets, but how did they manage it in the system?"

"Couldn't someone copy a student and move them to another grade?" I asked.

"Not exactly. The system auto-promotes students. If you manually move one backward or duplicate them, it flags inconsistencies."

Gertrude tilted her head as if she, too, found that suspicious.

I leaned closer to two identical names.

"Are these exactly the same students?"

We compared carefully.

"Middle initial missing here," Junie murmured.

"And here the birth month changed," I added. "Just by a few weeks."

Junie blinked.

"This one was listed in fifth grade... and also in kindergarten."

She let out a short laugh.

"Well, she must have been a prodigy preschooler and then spectacularly failed later."

"When was the last time a student repeated a grade?" I asked quietly.

Junie stopped smiling.

"Years. And it required district approval. Remember that transfer case? We had to override the system because the initial placement was incorrect."

I sat back slowly.

"They didn't create fake students," I said.

Junie looked at me.

"They recycled them."

Gertrude shuffled the stack with her beak, exposing more duplicates.

Real children.

Real IDs.

Slight alterations.

"They kept old records active," I continued. "Changed small details—birth months, initials—just enough to avoid automatic flags."

"And archived the paper copies," Junie added, nodding. "If someone checked the current grade folders, everything matches. I checked some of them."

"But no one noticed the repetition."

"Not everyone has your memory, Tony."

I smiled and nodded, but corrected her. "Junie, a girl named Athena would have caught your attention if you saw her more than once in the same year. I don't think this crossed your desk, or Harold's."

"Well, whoever did it really knows our office, Tony. That's scary."

We both grew quiet.

I began sorting by school.

"That's interesting," I murmured.

"What?"

"Only one school shows consistent 'growth.'"

Junie leaned over.

Lionel's Elementary.

Transfers in.

Enrollment increases.

Just enough to justify expansion.

"The other schools have fake transfers," I said. "But the enrollment balances out."

Junie frowned.

"So the duplication wasn't district-wide growth."

"No," I said slowly. "Harold got confused. This is linked to that elementary school, which probably means Lionel was behind it."

Gertrude gave a soft quack.

"Since the students had minimal changes, the system flagged nothing unusual. That's why Beatriz's study is technically clean," I said.

The students existed and belonged in the system.

They were simply counted twice.

I leaned back in my chair.

"Whoever did it had the confidence to assume no one would cross-check across grade levels," I said. "This wasn't sloppy."

"Not at all. It was genius!" Junie added.

Gertrude hopped down from the table and waddled toward the hallway, as if already ready for the next phase of investigation.

Junie exhaled slowly.

"So what does this mean?"

"It means," I said carefully, stacking the papers back together, "we need someone who can figure out where all this happened."

Junie frowned. "Where? Didn't we agree it all happened in the elementary school?"

"Not that. Like in which computer, Junie?" I gathered the documents neatly into the folder. "Anyone could sneak a fake file into a cabinet if we weren't looking. But logging into our system? That leaves a trail. Wallace always said digital footprints are stubborn things."

Junie stood up and put her hands on her hips. "And who knows how to do that, Tony?"

"We take this to Tricia," I stated as a matter of fact. "We explain how the fraud worked. And then we let her find out who had the access to pull it off."

Gertrude gave one decisive quack. I knew my limitations, and the computer world was one of them.

Junie refused to return to the police department.

Which I understood.

She had already spent most of the day there, waiting for me. And she was still afraid of being arrested.

I didn't say it aloud, but I was afraid too.

Alibi or not.

Gertrude and I walked into the station alone.

As we passed Tricia's office, I heard Arthur's voice from inside.

"Close," he was saying, "but not identical."

I slowed.

Gertrude did not. She waddled forward with the confidence of someone who had never once feared arrest.

I gently caught her before she pushed the door open.

"Toxicology shows cardiac glycosides consistent with digitalis in Lionel's blood," Arthur continued. "If you ask around, someone probably noticed he wasn't feeling well twenty-four to forty-eight hours before he died."

"And Marina?" Tricia asked.

"There were traces of the same toxin," Arthur replied. "But she had an underlying rhythm irregularity. Mild. Likely untreated. The toxin pushed her into cardiac arrest much faster. I'd estimate within an hour of ingestion."

Silence.

"As for the knife," Arthur added quietly, "I doubt Lionel even felt it. His heart had already given out. He was falling forward when someone pushed the blade into his back."

My breath caught.

Gertrude tilted her head and let out a soft, confused quack.

"So both victims were poisoned," Tricia said evenly.

"Yes."

"The mug in Miss Tony's office?"

"Same compound," Arthur answered. "The tea needs full analysis, but initial tests show digitalis."

Gertrude chose that moment to push the door open with her beak.

Both of them turned toward us.

"Miss Tony," Tricia said.

Arthur spun around. "Mom? What are you doing back here?"

I cleared my throat and stepped in fully, lifting the folder slightly like a peace offering.

"Chief Ben said it was fine," I said. "And I brought something."

Gertrude marched in ahead of me and parked herself beside Arthur's shoe.

Tricia stood behind her desk, arms folded.

"What is this, Miss Tony?"

I placed the thick report on her desk.

"Beatriz gave me this."

Tricia didn't say anything at first. She just

looked at me, using silence the way I often did. I had no choice but to keep going.

"This is the report Marina prepared for Lionel. Junie and I believe we've figured out how the fraud worked... if you're still interested in hearing about that."

Tricia picked up the folder, but of course it was Arthur who spoke first.

"How did you get Beatriz to hand that over? And how did she end up with it in the first place?"

"I went to see her," I said evenly. "Given how the evidence has been piling up around her, I thought it was worth the visit."

Arthur groaned.

But I didn't give him the chance to lecture me.

"Someone died in my office, Arthur Cooper," I said calmly. "I wasn't going to sit at home while you cleaned it up."

Tricia corrected without looking up, "Technically, the district is responsible for cleaning your office. Not us."

Of course, she was right. Beatriz had just told me so.

"That was a new rug!" I complained.

Gertrude quacked indignantly, as if in full agreement.

Tricia ignored us entirely.

"You said you figured out the fraud. Does that mean Beatriz and her company are cleared?"

"Absolutely not," I said before I could stop myself.

Both of them looked at me.

I softened my tone.

"I understand now why the study appears clean. The numbers match the system. The students are real. That's the trick."

Arthur leaned back slightly. "Explain."

"They didn't invent fake children," I said. "They reused real ones. A missing middle initial here. A birth month shifted there. Just enough to make the system treat them as different students."

Gertrude pecked once at the folder, as if confirming the math.

"Lionel's elementary school shows the only steady 'growth,'" I continued. "The other schools even out. His numbers justified the expansion—potentially unlocking significant grant funding."

Tricia's eyes sharpened.

"So the study analyzed flawed data."

"Yes," I said. "The study did its job. It just trusted numbers that had already been bent."

Arthur crossed his arms.

"And you're certain about this?"

"I've been in that district long enough to recognize every senior by face and half the middle schoolers by their handwriting," I replied. "These students exist. They were simply counted twice."

Tricia picked up the folder.

"So you think she did it?" Arthur asked.

I shook my head.

"No. I don't know. But I can't be certain she didn't."

I took a breath.

"I understand now why her company's study appears clean. But I also know she worked closely with Lionel. And according to her, Marina confronted her this morning—accused her outright. She seemed genuinely shocked when I told her Marina had died..."

I sighed.

"She also mentioned that Rita Carver argued with Lionel during several study meetings. Apparently, Rita and Lionel were involved. And there were rumors that Marina had an affair with him."

Tricia crossed her arms, but I continued before she could interrupt.

"When I spoke to Marina, she denied the

affair. She said she resigned because she was afraid of what she discovered in that report—and she didn't believe Harold would support her once the rumors started spreading."

I lowered my hands slowly.

"Harold confirmed he spoke with her. He tried to convince her to transfer to another school instead of quitting."

Tricia nodded and closed the folder.

"I'll send this to IT to trace the document history and filing sequence," she said. "Thank you, Miss Tony."

"What happens now?" I asked.

Arthur stepped aside as Tricia moved past him and out of the office. Gertrude and I followed close behind.

"We'll release Harold," she said, quickening her pace.

"I thought you were afraid for his life," I added.

Tricia stopped and turned to face me.

"I am," she said evenly. "But I no longer have grounds to hold him. Marina's death changes the circumstances. And this report"—she lifted the folder slightly—"pertains to fraud, not homicide."

Before I could respond, she pointed at me—not aggressively, but firmly.

"I will investigate the digital trail on this," she said. "And—against what most people would advise—I will share my findings with you."

I opened my mouth.

"If," she added, "you stop involving yourself in this fraud investigation."

My arms folded automatically across my chest.

I nodded.

Slowly.

"Thank you," she said, and walked away.

Arthur began a quiet speech about safety protocols and staying out of active investigations.

I barely heard him.

What I heard instead was the way she had said it.

Fraud investigation.

To me, that meant one thing.

She was still drawing a line between fraud and homicide.

And I had just been removed from the first one.

I still needed Rita's address.

It was probably time to get back to the town's insiders.

Chapter 16

I wasn't surprised to find Martha in the bakery talking to Prue. In fact, I had been counting on it.

Gertrude marched ahead of me toward the back table, hopped onto the bench, and quacked her displeasure at the delay in service, as if poor Prue had been personally responsible for our arrival.

"Well, hello to you too, Gertrude," Prue said with a laugh.

Gertrude flapped her wings for emphasis.

Martha slid a berry from her pavlova toward my bird. "Peace offering."

Gertrude accepted it with all the grace of a duck who believes she is owed tribute.

"Tony," Martha said, lowering her voice,

"how is the case going? We heard about Marina. Poor girl."

Of course they had.

I told them what we knew—or at least what I could share. They weren't involved in the fraud or the murder, and sometimes saying things aloud helped me hear what I had missed.

Arthur had been wonderful, but also protective. And with whatever tension still lingered between him and Tricia, I wasn't eager to complicate things further.

"It's such a mess," I finished. "Did you know Marina had a heart disorder?"

Prue returned with another sampler plate for Gertrude and set a cup of tea in front of me.

I hesitated.

I knew Prue hadn't poisoned anyone, but the memory of Arthur describing the toxin in the office mug made my stomach tighten.

"What is it, Tony?" Prue asked gently.

"It's just..." I lowered my voice. "Arthur found traces of the same toxin in the mug Junie gave Marina. That may be what killed her."

Martha covered her mouth. Prue gasped softly.

"What are we whispering about?"

I nearly jumped out of my skin.

Gladis Williams stood behind us, hands on her hips, entirely too pleased with herself. Like Martha, Agnes, and Prue, she had also been in our high school class. Now she owned the flower shop on Main Street and ran the town's gardening club.

Within minutes, she was up to date.

"And you want to talk to Rita now?" Gladis asked.

I nodded, finishing my tea. "She seemed closest to Lionel. And after what Beatriz mentioned, it makes sense."

"What about his children?" Prue asked.

I shook my head. "He didn't have any. There's an ex-wife, but she's out of the country. From what I've gathered, they weren't close. Honestly, Rita was the only one who looked truly heartbroken."

"Do you think the police will question her?" Martha asked.

"Maybe," I said. "But you know Rita. She won't open up easily. I'm hoping she might talk to me. I just need her address..."

Martha immediately shook her head. "Tony, you know I can't give out private information. What if an angry student asked for yours? It's a safety issue. And unethical."

"But this is murder—"

"You said poisoned?" Gladis interrupted me. "What kind of poison?"

I sighed, shaking my head. "Arthur said something about a toxin. Maybe digits or digitals?"

"You mean digitalis?" Gladis asked.

I nodded. "I think so. Why?"

Gladis adjusted her glasses. "You know foxglove? Beautiful tall bells, blooming in early summer—mainly purple. It's been all over the backyards since the city started that butterfly garden campaign two years ago."

We all nodded, which drew a bright smile from Gladis.

"It's also called *Digitalis purpurea*," she added, tilting her head slightly. "Highly poisonous."

Of course, she would know that.

Martha blinked. "Poisonous?"

"Yes," Gladis said matter-of-factly. "The plant contains cardiac compounds—I remember it better as digitalis. In small medical doses, it's used for heart conditions. In larger amounts? It can stop a heart altogether. That's why we always tell new members of the club not to let pets chew on it."

Gertrude froze mid-peck and slowly lifted her head.

"That puts it in virtually anyone's hands!" I exclaimed.

Gladis turned to me. "Well, it's terribly bitter, Tony. You'd notice right away if you tried to eat it... unless the culprit hid it behind something else, like a lot of honey or sugar."

I forced a small smile.

"Well," I said lightly, "I'll make sure Gertrude keeps her distance."

Gertrude quacked in protest.

"I can give you her address, though," Gladis said without hesitation.

"What about client-privacy privileges?" Martha asked, almost in shock.

"Oh, honestly, Martha—it's a murder. I think we can make an exception. And it won't be from my client list. I'm telling you this as her friend."

We all turned to her.

"What? She's in my gardening club. The woman loves her plants, just like me."

"Rita gardens?" I asked.

"Oh yes," Gladis said proudly. "Vegetables, roses, perennials. She's a frequent buyer at my shop, and I send flowers to her house quite often."

This time, my smile mirrored Gladis's pride.

This was getting somewhere.

I was just about to ring Rita's doorbell when I heard a car pull into the driveway behind me. The porch light cast a soft glow across the driveway, the kind that only made the night feel deeper.

I turned.

Tricia stepped out of the driver's side, closing the door with calm precision. I couldn't tell if she was relieved to see me—or satisfied to have found me exactly where she expected.

"Miss Tony," she said as she approached. "I thought you weren't particularly close with Miss Carver."

I frowned and crossed my arms. "Did Arthur tell you that?"

A faint smile tugged at her lips, but there was something weary behind it.

"You work in the school district," she said evenly. "Rita Carver is president of the Parents' Board. It doesn't take a detective to know that's not your favorite committee."

She glanced at the door. "Have you rung the bell?"

I shook my head and stepped aside, offering her the honor.

The doorbell chimed sweetly inside the house.

We waited.

Nothing.

She rang again. Then knocked.

Still nothing.

"She could be in the shower," I offered.

It wasn't entirely wishful thinking.

Wallace once told me about a case where no one answered the door. They finally broke it down, expecting the worst, only to find a poor woman enjoying her bathtub—wearing nothing but her natural embarrassment.

I used to roll my eyes at his stories.

Now, apparently, they lived rent-free in my head.

Still, I've always loved listening to them.

Even the ridiculous ones.

Tricia didn't answer me. She was already moving down the side of the house toward the backyard.

Gertrude waddled after her without hesitation.

I followed.

"Miss Tony!"

Her voice was sharp this time.

I sped up until I spotted her through the glass doors.

Rita lay sprawled on the kitchen floor.

Tricia tested the handle.

Locked.

She didn't hesitate.

She grabbed a patio chair and struck the glass near the latch. It shattered with a crack that made me jump.

"Call 911!" she ordered.

I fumbled for my phone as she stepped into the kitchen.

By the time I reached the doorway, Tricia had rolled Rita gently onto her back.

"She's breathing," she said, leaning close to Rita's face. "Shallow, but breathing."

My heart pounded so loudly I could barely hear the dispatcher when they answered.

"Emergency services," the operator said.

"Yes," I managed, forcing my voice steady. "We need an ambulance. Possible poisoning. Female, unconscious but breathing."

I repeated the address while Tricia checked Rita's pulse and scanned the counters.

Gertrude stood just outside the broken door, feathers puffed, unusually silent.

For once, she wasn't demanding food.

She was watching.
Waiting.
And so was I.

Chapter 17

The hospital looked different in the morning light—quieter, almost ordinary, as if the chaos of the night before had never happened at all.

Last night, it hadn't taken long for me to give my statement. Tricia had been with me the entire time, and the only real question was why I had been at Rita's house in the first place.

That was easy enough.

I needed to ask her about the report. And Lionel.

While I waited, I had scanned the house and yard, just in case. There were no signs of foxglove anywhere. Outside, it was still too early for most plants to push through the winter soil. Inside, she had magnificent bonsai and a spectacular orchid, but nothing tall, leafy, or bell-shaped.

Nothing that looked like early summer.

It had kept me up all night. So, with that in mind—and knowing Rita was very much a victim—I drove to the hospital first thing in the morning.

I was telling Gertrude to wait near the small garden outside the entrance—my sweet duck had never done well around sick people—when Penny Whitcomb stormed out of the sliding doors.

"Penny!" I called.

To my surprise, she stopped, turned, and marched straight toward me.

"Miss Tony," she said sharply. "I should have listened to you."

I nearly stepped back.

Those were words I never imagined hearing from Penny. And the defeated expression on her face was so sincere it almost unsettled me.

"What's wrong?" I asked, guiding her a few steps away from the entrance.

She glanced at her notebook, then snapped it shut and shoved it into her purse.

"All that work," she muttered. "All that digging. For nothing."

I waited.

“The fraud isn’t real,” she said, throwing her hands up. “It’s just a love triangle gone bad.”

Gertrude quacked softly beside me, as confused as I felt.

“A love triangle?” I repeated.

Penny groaned. Actually groaned.

“Yes, Tony. Or maybe a square. Who knows how many women Lionel was juggling? But that’s all this is.”

She blurted out her theory in a desperate rush.

“Lionel had an affair with Marina. Rita finds out. Rita tampers with the study to ruin his precious expansion project—the legacy he was so proud of. When Lionel confronts Marina instead of groveling, Rita snaps. She stabs him. Then she poisons Marina to tie up loose ends. And today?” She waved vaguely toward the hospital doors. “Another dramatic performance to misdirect the investigation.”

I stared at her.

“It’s outrageous! Do you think Rita would do this to herself?”

Penny crossed her arms. “She killed her lover and his affair. Yeah, I think she would.”

It was a dangerous theory. It sounded crazy, but to an outsider, it almost made sense.

"But the fraud is real," I said quietly. "Junie and I found duplicated students. Altered records. It's not imagined."

Penny rolled her eyes.

"Oh, Tony. Do you think I believe every government system is flawless? Of course there are issues. But the point of exposing this fraud was to prove something larger—that this town isn't as clean as it pretends to be. Even in the school district's department."

She leaned closer.

"And now? Now it's just jealousy and bad decisions."

"Two people are dead," I said. "One is fighting for her life. That's more than gossip."

Penny's expression hardened.

"My whistleblower," she said pointedly, "she's compromised now. Useless."

She started toward the parking lot.

I hurried after her.

"You need to tell the police," I insisted. "If you even suspect your source could be involved—"

She laughed.

"Oh, Tony. If I believed for one second that my whistleblower committed a crime, I would report her myself. And I would be there when she was arrested."

She adjusted her purse on her shoulder.

"This is simple. People fall in love. They get jealous. They make terrible choices. Not everything is a grand conspiracy."

"And that's going to be your story?" I asked.

She paused.

"I don't know yet," she said. "This won't sell as real investigative reporting. It's messy. Personal. And unlike what you believe, I do care about my reputation."

Then she walked away.

Gertrude let out a low quack.

I watched Penny's retreating figure and felt something tighten in my chest.

Penny was wrong.

But she had done something important without realizing it.

She had shown me how easily this could be explained away.

And whoever was truly behind this would be counting on exactly that.

I was surprised to find Arthur standing outside Rita's hospital room.

"Mom, are you all right?"

He pulled me into a hug—something I will accept anytime, even when it comes wrapped in overprotection.

"I'm fine," I said quickly. Then panic flickered through me. "Is Rita okay? Did she—"

"The doctors are working to flush the toxin from her system," he said, guiding me down the hallway. "They're assessing potential internal damage. She's still unconscious."

I didn't like that.

Somehow, I had imagined that Tricia and I had arrived just in time—that Rita would be sitting up already, apologizing for the drama.

It also explained why Penny had stormed out of the hospital.

She hadn't been able to get a statement.

"Is it the same toxin?" I asked.

Arthur gave me a long look before sighing—the sound of a man surrendering to inevitable maternal interrogation.

"Most likely. The symptoms are consistent," Arthur said. "But I need lab confirmation before I make anything official."

He hesitated a second, then added more quietly, "Whoever administered it knew what they were doing."

I crossed my arms. "Rita belongs to a gardening club. She would know about foxglove."

Arthur gave me a sideways look. "Why am I not surprised you know that?"

I ignored that.

"I have to ask," I said, lowering my voice, "do you think she poisoned herself?"

I didn't believe it—not truly—but the possibility floated in my mind, thanks to Penny.

"I can't tell whether she ingested it willingly," he said carefully. "But I can tell you this wasn't a trace exposure. The dose was deliberate. If you and Tricia hadn't arrived when you did, she wouldn't have survived."

That settled heavily between us.

Whoever had poisoned Lionel.

Whoever had poisoned Marina.

Had tried again.

And was still out there.

"I ran into Penny outside," I said, needing to shift the weight of that thought.

Arthur frowned. "I was hoping you'd miss her. She was upset. Not in a compassionate way." He shook his head. "Tricia's still at Rita's house, so Penny couldn't get comments from her. And certainly nothing from me. Did she accuse you of anything?"

I laughed softly. Penny and I had clashed before, but never like that.

"She's convinced this is a crime of passion," I said. "A love triangle gone wrong."

Arthur smirked as we walked toward the exit.

"That might make sense," he said slowly, "if the fraud wasn't involved. Wasn't her article centered on the fraud?"

"Yes," I replied. "But now she thinks the fraud might not be real. She believes her source could be compromised because of her relationship with the victims."

Arthur stopped walking.

"Do you know who the whistleblower is, Mom?"

"Of course not!" I moved past him, offended by the implication. "I would never protect that kind of information."

Lowering my voice, I added, "She let slip that it's a woman. That's all. I suspect Tricia has figured that out too."

"Beatriz," Arthur said quietly as he caught up to me. "You went to see her. She gave you the report."

I nodded as we reached my car.

"If she's the whistleblower, it would explain why she had the report," I said. "And her involvement with Lionel's school and the study could have pushed her to speak to Penny first—afraid the police would look at her company."

Arthur leaned against the car door before opening it for me.

"That might explain the report," he said carefully. "But if she's clean—if her company is clean—why not go directly to the police? She has nothing to lose."

That question lingered.

Then I remembered why I started all this in the first place.

"Harold," I said. "He was already being questioned. If your father were suspected of a crime, that alone might make me hesitate before going straight to the police. She may have been trying to clear him quietly. Harold doesn't think clearly under pressure. You should see him at the end of a semester."

Arthur chuckled despite himself.

Before closing the door, though, his tone shifted.

"Be careful, Mom. Dad's been gone a week, and you've already stumbled into two murders and an attempted one. Go back to work. Let Tricia handle the rest."

I reached up and patted his cheek.

"I'm always careful."

I didn't mention that going up against furious parents about their kids' education was far more terrifying than anything we dealt with this week.

Gertrude hopped into the passenger seat with a determined quack.

And despite everything, I smiled.

Chapter 18

Technically, I was working.

When I parked outside Harold's house, my intention was to discuss the school department—which, in my mind, absolutely counted as work. I had heard he'd been released that afternoon, and I couldn't let another day pass without checking on him.

"Tony!" he exclaimed, pulling me into a tight hug. "This is much better than the station. Please, come in."

Gertrude marched in ahead of me as though conducting an inspection.

I expected the messy living room from the day before—papers everywhere, takeout boxes stacked like small towers of defeat.

Instead, I found a clean house, and Harold led me straight to the kitchen.

Something simmered on the stove and smelled wonderful.

I had no intention of tasting it, though. If I'd been worried about getting busted in the shower, now I was paranoid about eating outside my house.

"Do you want something to—"

"No, thank you," I interrupted gently.

He nodded and sat on a stool at the counter. He still looked tired, but not hollow the way he had at the station. His cheeks had returned. His eyes were merely weary instead of haunted.

"It's good to see you home," I said. "The district has been dragging without you. We'll need to put things back in order."

His expression shifted.

"I don't think I'll be going back, Tony."

That caught me off guard.

"Beatriz wants to leave town," he continued. "She's been deeply affected by everything. The accusations... the whispers. People think she's involved in the fraud. In the murder." He swallowed. "She's sensitive. I just want her to be happy."

That felt... sudden.

"Are you at least waiting for the fraud to be

cleared?" I asked carefully. "And the investigation?"

"I will," he said, placing a full plate of food in front of himself but not touching it. "Beatriz is going to her sister's for a while. We'll figure out the rest."

His eyes drifted toward the closed office door down the hallway.

"She still doesn't want to go in there?" I asked.

A faint smile touched his lips. "At least I don't have to hear about my shoes on her expensive carpet anymore."

The carpet.

Something clicked.

"Wait," I said slowly. "Her carpet? Isn't that your office?"

He laughed. "Tony, that office is hers. I don't bring district work home. You know that. We've always made fun of people who do."

The room shifted under my feet.

I didn't ask permission.

I walked straight down the hall and opened the office door.

"Tony—"

I stepped inside, holding my breath. I could imagine how bad the place would have smelled, with traces of blood soaked into that carpet, if not for the windows thrown wide open to let the air in.

The office was spotlessly clean, though. Except for the dark stain on the carpet—faint, but visible.

And the rest of the room...

Empty.

No binders.

No paperwork.

No computer.

Nothing.

Even Gertrude paused in the doorway.

I opened a drawer.

Empty.

Another.

Empty.

"Harold," I said, my voice thinner than I intended. "When did she pack this?"

He stepped in behind me, confusion spreading across his face.

"I... I don't know."

Just like the living room yesterday, it had been chaos.

Now it was spotless.

Gertrude waddled past me and pecked at the edge of the carpet.

"Where is she?" I dared to ask.

"She had a massage appointment," Harold said weakly. "Her nerves, she said..."

Massage. Again.

While packing.

And this fast. I didn't think so.

"She's leaving you," I said before I could stop myself.

Harold's face crumpled. "No. She wouldn't."

"Harold, you were in prison until this afternoon, and she already packed?"

Harold shook his head. "She wouldn't—her plants."

He rushed to the living room and lifted a potted orchid as proof.

"See? She's coming back. She loves her plants... probably more than me, but that's not the point. She wouldn't leave them."

Plants.

Watering.

After the murder.

She had insisted on watering Harold's plants in the office.

She'd called it a fern.

Ferns don't need daily watering.

Even I knew that.

My stomach dropped.

She hadn't been watering plants.

She'd been trying to retrieve something.

A plant.

And this office was hers.

With the expensive carpet.

The one that didn't match the rest of the house.

And with access to Harold's things—including his office in the district.

"Harold," I said firmly. "We need to go. Now."

"To where?"

"City Hall."

Gertrude flapped her wings and hurried toward the door as if she understood the urgency.

I just hoped Beatriz hadn't been inside our offices yet.

Chapter 19

When I rushed out of Harold's house, practically dragging him with me, there were only two things on my mind: calling Arthur and that plant.

Nothing else mattered.

So when we found the department door open, I didn't think twice.

It wasn't until Harold pushed open the office door that my heart skipped.

Beatriz stood inside.

One hand wrapped tightly around a pot with a dry plant in it.

"What are you doing here?" she asked.

The shock on her face matched my own.

"Put the pot down," I said, stepping forward.

Harold instinctively blocked me and gently pushed me behind him.

Gertrude, however, marched past both of us and planted herself in the doorway, wings slightly out, issuing a low, offended quack.

"This doesn't concern you," Beatriz said coolly.

She tried to walk past Harold.

He didn't move.

"I want an explanation," he said. "I spent days in jail, accused of having killed my friend. Did you really kill—"

"Kill Lionel?" she finished for him.

Her smile was slow.

"Yes," she said. "And he had it coming. No one breaks up with me."

Harold physically staggered.

"Yes, Harold. Your friend," she continued, "he was having an affair with your wife. And we were happy. Very happy. Once he ended his marriage, hiding from only you became effortless."

My heart ached for Harold. For the last fifteen minutes, I had been convinced Beatriz was in on the fraud and murders, but I hadn't believed she was involved with Lionel.

"You're the whistleblower," I said. "And

you orchestrated the fraud. Did Marina ever even give you that report?"

Beatriz's eyes sparkled.

"Oh, Tony, I totally tricked you. Honestly, I thought you were sharper than that. A couple of wrong turns, and you were completely lost."

I opened my mouth, but she didn't let me say a word.

"Of course Marina didn't threaten me. I had nothing against her. It was Lionel who involved her when he used her to expose our fraud."

"Why would Lionel do that?" I asked.

"Revenge, I guess," she said. "He claimed he'd fallen in love with Rita. Rita." She scoffed. "I merely planted doubt in her mind. Lionel's reputation did the rest."

"If that's true, wouldn't that mean you already won? Why kill him after you'd ruined his relationship with Rita?"

Beatriz answered calmly, "Betrayal, Tony. He was mad I ruined his relationship, so he tried to cross me. I warned him that leaving me could lead to regret, but betrayal would have a price."

Harold's voice broke. "So you stabbed him? In our house?"

She laughed.

"Why would I make a mess in my own home? I didn't stab him."

"You just said you killed him! I had no idea who did that. I actually thought it was you, Harold."

That would have made sense. Lionel confesses the affair, Harold loses control, grabs the nearest knife, and—

But I had been there.

I had seen Harold when he found the body.

The shock in his eyes hadn't been anger. It hadn't been guilt. Devastation—the kind that comes from discovering a friend dead. Or like the one he had now.

"You said you killed him!" Harold shouted. "You just confessed!"

Beatriz sighed, lowering her tone as if she were explaining something painfully obvious.

"And this is why I found Lionel far more interesting than you, Harold. He had initiative. Not daydreams."

Then she snapped, "I poisoned him! Why do you think Tony wants this plant?"

Harold turned to me, confusion clouding his face.

I nodded once.

He clearly hadn't known about the poison.

I swallowed and forced myself to stay steady.

"So," I asked, keeping my voice even, "how did you get the report?"

Gertrude let out a low quack.

"Lionel was clever," Beatriz said smoothly. "He wanted to look noble in Rita's eyes. It didn't take a genius to realize he must have sent the report to her."

The satisfaction in her voice curved into a slow smirk.

"The blind woman never suspected me and Lionel. But I knew about them. We had tea yesterday morning and simply told her I could protect my company—and Harold—if she trusted me. She handed over the report without hesitation."

Gertrude gave a sharp, disapproving quack.

I frowned.

That only made Beatriz laugh.

"Then I gave you exactly the parts of the report I wanted you to see," she continued. "Your word, Tony, is gold in this town. If you couldn't find guilt in my company, no one would. Not even in the gray areas."

That really upset me. I could use that to my advantage, like I did with Penny, but no one should try to use my reputation to cover a crime. Especially murder.

"And then you killed Marina?" I asked, disgust tightening my voice. "Because you knew I would talk to her? That she would tell me everything? Tell me—did she figure out your affair?"

Beatriz's eyes flicked toward me—just a flash.

"I did not kill Marina," she said coolly. "I didn't even know she had tried to speak to you until she was found dead in your office."

Gertrude tilted her head sharply.

"I'm sure Junie poisoned her," Beatriz added lightly. "When she came to see you."

"Junie has nothing to do with this!"

Beatriz laughed again.

"Oh, I know she doesn't. She's naive. And kind. Did she offer Marina something to drink? She always does when I visit."

I didn't answer.

I didn't need to.

"See?" Beatriz pressed. "I figured that one out in a second. Junie accidentally poisoned her by using Harold's mug."

Gertrude's feathers ruffled.

I turned slowly toward Harold.

The way he had looked in jail. Pale. Weak. Then suddenly better.

It made a sick kind of sense.

"You were poisoning me?" Harold whispered.

"Not to kill you," Beatriz said. "I needed to test the dosage. I couldn't risk killing Lionel without precision."

Gertrude lunged forward and pecked hard at the edge of the pot in Beatriz's hands.

"The massage appointment," I said, shaking my head. "Your alibi."

She smiled.

"It doesn't matter anymore," I said firmly. "We will tell the police—"

Her smile didn't fade.

My nerves tightened.

"No, you won't," she said, stepping toward me. "There's no recording of this conversation. You have my emotionally unstable husband, who just discovered I was having an affair with the man who betrayed his confidence and manipulated the school district."

"And you, Tony... you just want to protect Junie."

Her smile didn't reach her eyes.

"Your best friend. The one working with

Lionel on the fraud. The one who accidentally killed Marina while experimenting on Harold."

She tilted her head.

"And when she realized Lionel might have told Rita something... she acted. A thoughtful little gift basket. Poisoned tea included."

Gertrude hissed—an unmistakably hostile sound.

I planted my hands on my hips.

"You can't prove that."

"Oh, I can," Beatriz said softly. "Do you think I came here only for this plant? Which, by the way, isn't even the one you were looking for."

My stomach dropped.

"Don't tell me you missed the one behind Junie's desk."

"That's not foxglove," I shot back. "It's an orchid."

And then it clicked.

The orchid in her house.

The orchid in Rita's house.

"Silly, Tony," she said. "You don't need the entire plant. Dry stems. Leaves. Even petals. Grind them. Hide them in soil. Orchids are perfect cover—the soil is loose and dark."

Beatriz's composure tightened.

"You open your mouth," she hissed,

pointing at me again, "and I destroy Junie. I will testify she poisoned Lionel. I'll say she targeted Harold. I'll say she panicked and tried to silence Rita. This town will believe it."

Harold looked at me—broken, defeated.

Gertrude stepped closer to my side, feathers lifted, guarding.

The frustration of being so close to the truth tightened my throat.

Almost enough to make me cry.

Almost.

"That was a good plan," Tricia said as she stepped into the office, gun raised and steady. "Too bad I had to ruin it."

I turned.

At least fivc more officers followed her inside.

I couldn't hide my smile—especially when I saw Beatriz's expression shift. The confidence drained slowly, like water finding a crack.

"Beatriz Wilkins," Tricia continued, snapping handcuffs around her wrists, "you are under arrest for the murder of Lionel Hudson. You have the right to remain silent..."

She went on with the Miranda rights, but I barely heard a word.

Arthur walked into the office.

He didn't hesitate—he pulled me into a hug so tight I had to push at his chest.

"Arthur," I protested, "you're going to crack a rib."

He loosened his grip but kept his hands firmly on my shoulders.

"Are you all right, Mom? I was at the hospital when you called. Luckily, Tricia was already on her way to the station. You should have waited—"

"If I had waited," I cut in, "Junie would have been framed for murder."

He sighed.

He knew I was right.

"And I did call you," I added. "You are part of the police, aren't you?"

He opened his mouth—then wisely closed it.

Behind us, Tricia guided Beatriz toward the hallway. Beatriz walked stiffly now, all arrogance gone.

Gertrude waddled forward and gave a sharp, victorious quack as Beatriz passed.

Tricia paused in front of me.

I braced for a reprimand.

Instead, her voice softened.

"Miss Tony, would you mind taking Harold to the hospital? It would be wise to assess how much damage the poison may have caused."

I looked toward Harold.

He was sitting on the edge of a chair, his head buried in his hands. Smaller, somehow.

"I asked him to go," Tricia continued quietly, "but he refused. I can't force him... but perhaps you can convince him."

Gertrude was already at Harold's feet, nudging his ankle gently with her beak.

"Absolutely," I said. "I'll take him now."

Tricia nodded once and continued down the hallway.

She didn't look at Arthur.

The air between them tightened in a way only a mother notices.

As soon as she disappeared around the corner, I punched Arthur lightly in the shoulder.

"Ow—Mom!" he complained. "What was that for?"

"I don't know what you did," I said firmly, "but you will apologize, Arthur Cooper."

He blinked at me.

"She is a good girl. And you will behave like the gentleman I raised."

Arthur rubbed his shoulder and muttered something about professional boundaries, but I was already walking toward Harold.

I didn't quite know when I had grown so fond of Tricia, but I was certain she would be good for my boy—that is, if he had the sense to mend whatever foolish thing he had done.

Gertrude gave an approving quack and led the way.

Chapter 20

My sweet Gertrude, of course, hadn't come inside the hospital. She preferred to wait outside by the small gardens, where she immediately began inspecting the flowerbeds with the seriousness of a very dedicated gardener.

It didn't take long for the doctors to reach a conclusion. They decided to keep Harold under observation for the next couple of days. Apparently, the poison may have affected some of his organs, but their main concern—and mine—was the shock his life had taken.

I could only imagine what it must feel like to learn that the spouse of decades had been cheating on you, had become a murderer, and had used you as a guinea pig to make sure the poison worked.

On my way out, I decided to ask for an update on Rita's condition. Turns out I was on her visitor list, so I swung by. After everything she had been through, I suspected she might want someone to talk to.

I was right.

"Hi, Rita," I said as I peeked into her room. "I was just—"

"Tony!" she exclaimed from the bed in the middle of the room. "Please, come in."

I stepped inside carefully, making sure not to bump any of the equipment surrounding her bed.

"Thank you for saving my life," she said.

I shook my head quickly. "It was Detective Tricia who actually saved you. I was there, but—"

"Thank you, Tony," she insisted softly before sighing. "The doctor told me the police want to talk to me, but they haven't come yet. And I honestly don't understand what happened."

After everything I had just learned, I figured I should go easy on the truth here.

"Do you remember Beatriz visiting you?"

Rita's expression hardened.

"Yes. She came yesterday—early in the morning. She said—"

Tears rolled down her cheeks. I reached out and gently touched her hand. I was about to tell her the truth about Beatriz, but she spoke first.

"It was me, Tony," she burst out.

Between sobs, she continued.

"I killed Lionel."

I sat back, stunned.

Before I could even process it, the words poured out of her.

"I knew Lionel was having an affair, but I didn't know with whom. So I started looking into it. I thought it was Beatriz... but I was wrong, Tony."

She wiped her eyes and took a shaky breath.

"Things had been going so well between us. A few weeks ago, he seemed happier. Lighter. But then the rumors about him and Marina started. Despite our breakup, I had to find out. I didn't believe it was her. So I followed him."

Her voice trembled.

"I was shocked when he opened Beatriz's door with a key. Suddenly everything made sense—the late meetings about the study, the secrecy, Marina quitting after working on that enrollment report."

Her eyes lowered.

"I followed him inside. He was acting strange. I think he was drunk. Then he pulled me so hard, it was painful. I pushed him and ran out of the kitchen. I don't remember grabbing the knife."

She looked at me with eyes full of pain.

"When he stumbled into the office, I panicked. I thought he was going to hurt me. He was groaning and mumbling. His eyes looked... wrong. I hid behind the desk, and when he came closer, I rushed around and—"

Her voice broke.

"I don't even know how the knife went in. I just saw him fall. Then I heard Harold's voice—" She covered her face with her hands. "I ran."

"I believed the affair until Beatriz came to see me. She was so worried about Harold and the fraud, saying everything had been misunderstood. She even brought a gift basket with some teas and chocolates because she heard about my relationship with Lionel. I wasn't family, so I had nothing to do with the funeral arrangements. She seemed so kind... I can't believe I thought she could have—"

I gently squeezed her hands, stopping her.

I couldn't let her carry guilt that wasn't hers.

"Rita," I said softly, "you were right."

She stared at me, confused, shaking her head slowly.

"Beatriz was having an affair with Lionel," I explained. "When he ended it, she started the rumors about Marina. And when he decided to expose the fraud, she poisoned him."

Rita blinked in disbelief.

"She wanted the report," I continued. "She figured Lionel had given it to you. And when she visited, she twisted the truth so you would hand it to her."

Rita's mouth opened, but she didn't answer.

"She poisoned you too," I said. "And Lionel. That's why he was acting so strangely in the house that night. If I had to guess, he was trying to leave evidence to expose her fraud."

"Lionel was—no," Rita whispered. "I stabbed him. I killed him. I thought he was going to hurt me."

I tilted my head gently.

"Rita," I said softly, "my son Arthur—the medical examiner—determined that Lionel was likely already dead by the time the knife struck him. He doesn't believe Lionel even felt it."

Her eyes widened.

"You didn't kill him," I finished quietly. "Beatriz did."

Rita broke into tears.

But this time they sounded different.

Not like guilt.

More like grief finally allowed to breathe.

I stayed with her until Tricia arrived to take her statement. I wasn't sure what the legal consequences would be for Rita, but at least now we finally knew the truth.

And I had been right.

Harold and Junie had nothing to do with any of it.

Fraud Scheme and Murder Investigation Rock Apple Creek Schools

By Penelope "Penny" Whitcomb
Apple Creek Gazette

APPLE CREEK — What began as questions about school enrollment numbers has culminated in a murder investigation, a poisoning case, and the exposure of a deliberate data manipulation scheme that misrepresented student growth at Creek Elementary School.

Police confirmed late Saturday that Beatriz Wilkins, owner of Independent Educational Planning & Community Outreach and wife of School District Superintendent Harold P. Wilkins, has been arrested in connection with the death of elementary school principal Lionel Hudson.

According to police sources, Rita Carver, president of the Apple Creek Parents Advisory Board, encountered Hudson inside a private residence late Wednesday afternoon and believed she was acting in self-defense during a confrontation.

Authorities say Hudson had already been poisoned with a cardiac toxin prior to the stabbing.

Carver, who later survived a separate poisoning attempt linked to the same suspect, is recovering at Apple Creek Regional Hospital and is cooperating with investigators.

The investigation widened after Marina Lopez, a former teacher who had been reviewing enrollment records tied to the district's expansion study, died shortly after meeting with district officials. Police now believe her death was also caused by exposure to the same toxin.

Despite the scale of the manipulation, early findings suggest the broader Apple Creek School District was not directly involved in the scheme.

City officials announced that an independent review of enrollment records will begin immediately. Superintendent Harold Wilkins, who had previously been detained during the investigation, has since been cleared of involvement and is currently recovering in the hospital after investigators determined he had also been unknowingly exposed to the toxin.

The district has confirmed that Junie McCarthy, enrollment coordinator for Apple Creek Schools, will oversee a full audit and correction of district student records.

Meanwhile, Sue Williams, newly appointed

principal of Creek Elementary School, will work with district officials to stabilize operations while the investigation concludes.

Mayor Henry Dosal addressed the situation briefly Saturday evening.

"Apple Creek families deserve accurate information about their schools," Dosal said. "While investigators have determined the district itself was not responsible for the manipulation, we must examine how irregularities of this magnitude were able to continue without earlier detection."

Parents expressed relief that the district appears uninvolved in the criminal activity, but frustration that the issue went unnoticed for so long.

"Someone was clearly manipulating records," said one parent outside City Hall. "How did it take a murder investigation to uncover it?"

Officials acknowledged that several key observations made by members of the community helped investigators identify inconsistencies in the enrollment data early in the case. While authorities declined to name those individuals, one source involved in the investigation noted that certain details were first identified outside official channels—an uncomfortable reminder that irregularities within the system may have persisted longer than they should have.

City employees present at the time also confirmed that the meeting briefly attracted the attention of an unusual onlooker from the hallway, though investigators declined to comment on whether the bird had any role in the discovery.

Police say additional charges related to fraud and attempted murder are expected as the investigation continues.

While the town may soon see its enrollment numbers corrected, the larger questions remains: how a manipulation of school records escalated into one of the most disturbing criminal cases Apple Creek has faced in decades, and how long the scheme might have continued if not for this series of increasingly alarming events.

The Gazette will continue to follow the investigation as more details become available.

Epilogue

"Well, I can't say I'm surprised, Junie."

I said it as I walked into my office the morning after the council cleared the School District of any fraud.

Personally, although still slightly shocked, I agreed with the council and was pleased with the quick response from the city and the police. I won't deny I was biased. My son had done an excellent job, Tricia had turned out to be a remarkable detective who wasn't afraid to ask for help, and of course my dear friends were innocent.

Just the way I liked it.

Gertrude waddled in behind me as if she owned the place, inspecting the hallway carpet before settling beside Junie's desk.

"I thought Penny would be nicer," Junie said, taking a sip of her coffee. "After all, she kind of started this entire mess. And she didn't even apologize for the whistleblower situation. Using a murderer as an informant."

I chuckled as I walked toward my office.

I had known Penny for a long time. She was not the kind of person who admitted mistakes.

Neither was I, but that didn't matter.

I was rarely wrong.

Gertrude gave a satisfied little quack, as if she agreed.

On my desk, I noticed an invitation from the high school. Apparently, they were naming the Coach of the Year and throwing a celebration afterward. Of course I had been invited, since I worked closely with most of the teachers—and quite a few of the students—in that section of the district.

It would be nice to attend a celebration for a change.

After all, what could possibly go wrong?

Gertrude hopped onto the visitor's chair and began preening her feathers with suspicious enthusiasm.

A soft knock at the door drew my attention.

"Hi, Arthur," I said, genuinely happy to see him. "Do you need my help with a case or something?"

He shook his head as he stepped inside.

"No, Mom. In fact, you need to stay away from the police department."

I waved a dismissive hand at him. I had a natural talent for these things. His father knew it. Arthur really should have accepted that by now.

"So, what is going on?"

Arthur rubbed the back of his neck and frowned.

"Well... I was hoping—wondering if you would be okay if I invited someone to dinner."

I narrowed my eyes.

"You don't need my permission for that."

"Well... I kind of do," he admitted. "Since I'm living with you now. And it is your house."

I smiled warmly.

"Our house. May I know who this guest is?"

He didn't need to answer.

The sudden color rising to his face—and the way he began acting like my teenage son again—told me everything.

"Tricia," I said with a satisfied smile.

"It's not like that, Mom," he sighed, dropping into the chair across from me. "She's studying for a forensic exam, and I offered to help her after work. She also wants—" he cleared his throat. "I'm not sure about this, but..."

"Arthur?"

He rushed the rest out in one breath.

"She wants to talk to you about intuition in investigations. You made quite an impression on her, and she'd like to know how you developed—"

I burst out laughing.

Gertrude quacked loudly beside Arthur's chair, which did not help his dignity.

"Mom!"

"I knew she was smart."

Arthur stood up and shook his head.

"No, you didn't. You actually hated her when you first met her."

I frowned.

"I did not, Arthur Cooper."

My son was saved from a more serious confrontation thanks to my phone.

I answered just as Arthur escaped the room, still chuckling.

The calm, familiar voice of my husband greeted me on the other end.

"Hey there, pretty lady. How was your week?"

I watched Arthur give me a small wave before disappearing down the hallway as I settled comfortably into my chair—in my newly carpeted office.

"Wallace," I said, smiling. "Let me tell you what just happened... but first—how is Douglas?"

Gertrude quacked and settled comfortably on the corner of my desk, clearly expecting the full report.

And knowing Apple Creek, I had a feeling it wouldn't be long before we were both needed again.

I hope you enjoyed this charming prequel mystery in the Apple Creek School District Mysteries. If you would like to know when and how Miss Tony met Gertrude, you can find your free prequel here or visit my website: www.montiered.com

Acknowledgments

For your patience, support, belief in the cause, staying with me and tolerating the time that I took away from all of you to sit down and write. During these years, I learned so much from all of you. For listening to my stories, complaints, and successes. For your help and critiques, for all of these and more,

To Each one of you, who loves to read mysteries and took the time to read my take on them. My amazing coaches; Scarlett and Bryan, my mystery group friends, Mom, Gloria, Teddy, Josephine, and You up there...

Thank you.

About the Author

Hi, I'm Montie Red, and I have a not-so-secret addiction to crafting twists, turns, and mysteries best solved with a cup of tea (or maybe a snack). My mysteries series are inspired by my love for quirky small-town charm, meddling sleuths, and the occasional murder that needs unraveling—purely fictional ones, of course!

My biggest motivation is my amazing daughter, who keeps me inspired and grounded. We share our home with two lovable dogs, five chatty birds, and a husband who frequently attempts daring escapes from my writing world—usually by pretending there's a very important game to watch or a mandatory tee time.

When I'm not diving into cozy mysteries, I step through portals to other worlds, writing sci-fi and fantasy adventures under the pen name Monica Red. Whether it's catching a killer or navigating interstellar chaos, I'm always in the thick of an exciting tale.

Thanks for joining me on this storytelling journey. Grab a cozy blanket, dive into a book, and let's solve some mysteries together!

www.ingramcontent.com/pod-product-compliance
Lightning Source LLC
LaVergne TN
LVHW030919080826
845145LV00013B/2974

9781962293167